I0653597

Anastasia Redeemed

Time for everything

Trophy D'Souza

Published by New Generation Publishing in 2013

Copyright © Trophy D'Souza 2013

First Edition

The author asserts the moral right under the Copyright,
Designs and Patents Act 1988 to be identified as the author
of this work.

All Rights reserved. No part of this publication may be
reproduced, stored in a retrieval system or transmitted, in any
form or by any means without the prior consent of the author,
nor be otherwise circulated in any form of binding or cover
other than that which it is published and without a similar
condition being imposed on the subsequent purchaser.

www.newgeneration-publishing.com

 New Generation **Publishing**

DEDICATION

*This book is dedicated to
the People of Africa,
my Friends in Africa,
my former Colleagues in Africa and
the People I worked for in Africa.
Africa has inspired me and
has enriched my outlook on life.
I hope this book will help people
not familiar with Africa
to see people in Africa
in a new light.*

DISCLAIMER

The book is a work of fiction. The possible association of individuals, groups or institutions with characters or situations in the story is unintentional. The objectives of the story are to motivate and to inspire. There is no desire to cast aspersions at individuals or organizations, to challenge beliefs or to depreciate generally accepted values. All the writing is creative and original and there is no intended attempt to plagiarise published works or to infringe copyright laws.

ACKNOWLEDGEMENTS

*Thanks to New Generation Publishing for all the assistance to publish the book.

*Thanks to all my Reviewers who have taken time to read through the story. They have made extremely useful comments that have helped improve the quality of the book:

Fred Gomes (Brisbane, Australia), Xavier Pinto (Toronto, Canada), Sabita Nazareth (Goa, India), Joe Thompson (East Africa), Beena Menon (Pune, India), Bia Menezes (New York, USA), Phil Mathews (NE India), Joseph P Lazar (East Africa), Paul D'Souza (Toronto, Canada).

*Thanks to friends of mine who helped with the proof-reading and with other suggestions for the book, and for their encouragement and support.

*Thanks to Wikipedia for details and for the map of Kenya taken from its websites.

PREFACE

The six years I spent in Africa, mainly Tanzania in East Africa, setting up youth projects and a support network with other Education Services in the region, have left a positive impression on my outlook on life and on the work I did in subsequent years. I hope that this book will help in sharing some of those values with like-minded thinkers, writers and achievers.

An African Proverb says, 'A family is like a forest: when you are outside it is dense, when you are inside you see that each tree has its place.' I hope that this story set in an African context will help people who are 'outside' Africa see how meaningful is this rich tapestry where everything indeed 'has its place'. Political instability in some parts of Africa and economic fragility in others are not the true indicators of the great cultural and human wealth the continent offers.

Another African Proverb aptly says, 'If you close your eyes to facts, you will learn through accidents'. That is indeed possibly what many of the adventurers and colonialists did. Their selfish motives nearly destroyed entire peoples but they could not touch the resilience of the African human spirit.

A Swahili saying indeed confirms that, 'When two elephants fight, it is the grass that gets trampled'. These 'elephants' who scrambled for possession of African territory and dominance never really affected the people (grass). The grass is green again, and Africa is moving ahead in spite of all the 'teething' problems of development and progress. Perhaps what Africa needs today is a sense of unity in trying to move forward with one voice. Another African Proverb supports this suggestion, 'Cross the river in a crowd and the crocodile won't eat you.' Good luck Africa!

Trophy D'Souza

FOREWORD

The story is an interesting narrative – an insight into Anastasia's stream of consciousness - a riveting account of her life, firmly rooted in Akamba and Christian traditions brought alive against the exotic canvas of Africa. Anastasia's evolution from an innocent child, into a lovely, sensitive and strong woman, is through a maze of bewildering experiences.

Anastasia finds the members of the religious Order, whom she'd naively believed would help her in her quest of God and who are supposedly wedded to religion, surreptitiously enjoying the very pleasures forbidden to them. Her disillusionment is complete when she finds out that those who have the power and the right to stop her from her chosen path are themselves of flawed morals. Her disbelief is further compounded when she sees that these very 'guilty' people sit in justice over people who are normal, innocent, simple, honest and human.

Paradoxically, and despite the injustice meted out to her, Anastasia does not feel emotionally separated from her 'God'. She has a touching connection with Him, Who, while not seeming to look out for her and Who seems to be a bystander to her trials, does appear to be protecting her as her life pans out. There's a poignant critique of religious Orders as flawed and commercialised institutions of faith versus faith which is an intimate and personal connection with a supreme entity.

Anastasia's trials with facing the loss of her family, with living up to her brave decision to stick with Akamba tradition and with accepting her fatherless child have been presented through a sensitively crafted narrative, which seems to speak to the reader from deep within Anastasia's being. It is as if her voice grows, from that of a little girl with a simple and naïve perspective of the world and from that of a young woman in her quest of the Almighty, into a strong woman who has matured through the challenges life has thrown at her.

An easy read and a compelling book!

Beena Menon Training Consultant: Teacher Education - British Council, India

REVIEWS

The story is truly gripping, full of the realities that life throws up: challenges, pressures, tensions, opportunities, friendships, love and forgiveness. The Author uses his inimitable style to blend the African setting, so well described tied up with its own complexities and cultural nuances, into the Christian influences that seem to guide the outcomes. The childlike trust of the protagonist is the sustaining pillar that keeps her spirit vibrant and alive, and in the end offers her a tangible reward, her own offspring, 'Faith'. Anastasia, here, does almost a reversal role of Sudha, in the Author's second book (*The Singh Saga*). Both characters, very deftly handled by the Author, are aware of what is happening around them. However while Anastasia in many ways is the victim of circumstances Sudha would appear to be in control. In the end both come good in stories that offer resolution, and perhaps inspiration, in complicated human situations.

This book is also a significant contribution particularly to religious writing, offering trainers in religious Orders guidelines on how aware they should be in dealing with human and cultural sensitivities. In a world where even religious managers seem to succumb to the human weakness of manipulating situations to suit their own objectives (as the Author also exposed in his first book, *A Bumpy Ride*), the heroine of our story (*Anastasia Redeemed*) stays by the great truths of honesty and simplicity. The average reader too should find inspiration in this book which shows how Gospel values can help transform failure and trial into success and triumph with belief in self and trust in God.

Fred Gomes Education/Language Consultant, Queensland, Australia

The Author's perceptive insights into the traditions and culture of the Akamba make the story interesting and believable. The book shows how the influence of tribal traditions and of Christian influences in Africa can affect lives like Anna's. However the Author probably wanted Anna to speak more about how she became a victim of 'religious' managerial incompetence, as indeed did 'Ralph' earlier, in his first book (*A Bumpy Ride*). Both faced unbelievable discrimination. The motivational message of redemption comes across in both stories, though, while Ralph pulls it off, Anastasia succumbs, in the world of religious prestige, though she is finally 'redeemed'. Yet both show greater generosity of spirit than their religious managers, in spite of humiliating circumstances in their lives. *Anastasia Redeemed* is a must-read especially for trainers and trainees in religious Orders.

Sabita Nazareth Consultant/Counsellor: Parish Services, Goa, India.

The book has a narrative that grips you from the very start, and as a reader you want to empathise with Anna, not sure if you would have the gumption to be in Anna's shoes. It gets really exciting towards the middle of the book when she has to go through all those humiliating exchanges with her religious Manager. The Biblical flavour, in the titles to the chapters, so aptly chosen, adds as much to the suspense as to the resolution of the conflict. Yet there is an easy flow to

11

the story, set in all the richness of the Akamba background, so well described. However, the powerful message is really for religious Managers who don't seem to get their act together. The book is certainly a good read as much for trainer-managers as for trainees, as it offers explanations and solutions. For those who may find the Christian settings difficult to understand the Glossary is an excellent guide.

Xavier Pinto Consultant: Hospitality & Tourism Services, Toronto, Canada

The book gives a realistic picture of how a determined person can face up to life's challenges with courage and hope. Anastasia is an inspiration for mothers who have to encounter unavoidable realities. Her faith in the face of challenging circumstances is powerful motivation to women in similar situations. The Author, in his third book, takes us through an interesting African journey steeped in Kenyan culture in quite an absorbing way, blending the facts almost imperceptibly into a fascinating setting. His second book (*The Singh Saga*) also does something very similar, when the narrative takes you on a journey of human intrigue and manipulation through the Himalayan hills. I read '*Anastasia Redeemed*' in one sitting! I would highly recommend the book as much to Trainers as to Trainees in religious as well as in other circles.

Joe Thomson Consultant/Advisor: Youth Pastoral Services, East Africa

The story is well set into the background of Africa that does not seem to be as 'dark' as it is believed to be. American, Canadian, European and Asian cultural hang-ups don't really prove to be any different, except perhaps that the facts in *Anastasia Redeemed* happened at a time when a more news-conscious world was not as active. Today with Facebook, Twitter, the other social sites and the global media going viral or investigative on everything 'African', it would be quite an effort to 'redeem' Anastasia. The story, in sharp contrast, speaks of normal life, with all its ups and downs, coming across to the reader as just part of a human situation. This of course should not let the insensitive religious Managers off the hook. They need to tidy up their house. It is almost like non-Africans causing problems in Africa, again! One would have thought that this had stopped a century ago. Anastasia needs a hearing. She is eloquent, and the story is absorbing. It is really worth a read. It may help you think different.

Paul D'Souza Consultant: Education/Language, Toronto, Canada

This is a fabulous story that I felt compelled to read at one sitting. It is a thriller in more ways than one as it has a beautiful way of expressing profound truths in very interesting and easy-to-understand language. The book deals very openly with issues like human relationships even in religious circles, and so lets the reader get drawn into the story. Without undervaluing absolute truths or beliefs the book uses artistic licence and 'user-friendly' jargon to deal with many of these human realities: love, forgiveness, happiness, humour, sensuality, family, relationships, culture and prayer. There is a lot of content packed into this slender volume, rich in substance and quality, always conveying a motivational message. The Author's wide experience has helped make *Anastasia Redeemed* a worthwhile read in any continent, not just in Africa. The African setting though is revealing and inspiring.

Phil Mathews Consultant/Trainer: Youth Ministries, North India

This is a well-written nostalgic piece about life in Africa. This book provides a window into the world of Kenya in Africa. Some of the facts might be amazing especially to the non-African reader but are worth exploring: how a pregnancy is valued as a blessing, how every child is considered to be a gift from God, how elders are respected. The book also sensitively explores beliefs and practices in this part of the world. The typical 'western' reader, immersed in a hi-tech world, should relish this exotic experience presented in an easy-to-read style.

Bia Menezes Media/Library Specialist, New York, USA

Anastasia Redeemed is a very realistic life story of a young Kenyan woman whose life could inspire many young people to keep working at their ideals in life. The book describes her search for meaning in life by staying close to her culture, and by adhering to the spiritual values of her religion. The author shows good insights into the thinking, the customs and the psychology typical of the area. Noteworthy is the spiritual search of Anastasia that is highlighted through the complaint form of dialogues with her God. The story reveals several true but hidden realities of life in East Africa.

Joseph P Lazar Consultant/Trainer: Religious Training Services, East Africa

Contents

Anastasia Redeemed

Time for everything

Chapter 1: A time to be born: When it all began

We were the family that everyone noticed or at least talked about. We weren't really in the gossip columns but we must certainly have been in the limelight in the village for many reasons. Apart from being the centre of attention we were probably also trend-setters.

'She looks cute in that head scarf, doesn't she?' I overheard one scarf-spotter saying, when I was just about five, as Mum took me to Primary School early one winter morning. 'The boy's wearing new jeans as well,' was her gossipy neighbour's comment, when they noticed me in the local market with my eldest brother, Alwyn. 'I wonder how they do it. I wish I could afford to keep up with the latest trends.'

'Her father's the 'Bwana Mkubwa' (meaning 'big man' or Head/Leader in Kiswahili®) anyway. He'll surely know how to keep ahead of the race,' was the comment of another somewhat envious leading man of the village, Mr Kelele.

'What race are you talking of?' asked his rather simplistic pub mate, Mr Kinyua.

'Oh, it's just the drive that our Bwana Mkubwa has to keep pushing his family on to fame and.... fortune. Most of us just don't have the means to do that.'

'Now, that's a bit too much,' said Kinyua. 'Henry Mwamba is a good man. He works hard and looks after his family. If he makes an honest buck along the way, you can't grudge him that. He wouldn't do anything dodgy. The Mwambas are good people.'

Dad was the Headmaster of the little school, in what you would call a hamlet, on the borders of Mavoko®

town, not far from the larger town of Machakos®, in Kenya®, the heartland of the Akamba®, only about 200 km south of Nairobi, the capital of Kenya. My family and clan were Akamba, possibly the fourth largest group in Kenya, speaking Kikamba® which appears to have developed from the language of the Bantu®. The Bantu (people and language) probably originated in Nigeria or Cameroon in West Africa. It is interesting that several African languages especially south of the Sahara desert have their roots in Bantu, including Kiswahili and Kikamba.

Dad was educated in leading Christian® institutions and took in whatever 'western' education offered, especially a fluency in using English for his work and for communication. He was aware of his roots and besides speaking Kikamba he also spoke fluent Kiswahili, the language spoken in nine countries in East Africa, which in population terms is nearly a quarter of Africa. Kiswahili too, which in its purest form is a coastal language, developed because of the trade the Bantu had with the Arab traders, mainly those from Oman in the Middle East. There is evidence to show that some Akamba people, probably some of those who had moved closer to the Kenyan coast, traded with these Arab tradesmen who came in on their Dhows, or large boats. I know Dad did not deal with these traders, but I remember him bringing in some trinkets for me or Mum that had mother-of-pearl on them. I now know that he had bought them possibly from some of these traders.

Dad had got to that position, of being 'Bwana Mkubwa' in his work and in society, a long time before I was born. He was a respected figure in the tribal hierarchy as well as in the broader Christian population.

I speak of a 'broader' Christian church because, though we were strictly part of the Catholic® group, we stood for the same values as other Christian believers like the Methodists®, the Anglicans® and others. Dad attended local cultural functions in the area and was a leading member of the Akamba tribal group that met for regular chats or meetings, to decide on community or village matters. He also happened to be one of the prominent Catholics in the Church, and was in the Parish Council® which decided on programmes for the Parish and the Christian community. So, as Kelele put it, my father was indeed quite appropriately known as the 'Bwana Mkubwa'.

The village folk weren't really surprised at the comments of Kelele (whose name incidentally means 'noise maker') because he came across as one who seldom had anything nice to say about people. He often bragged about what he could do but he never really did anything constructive for the village. Kinyua on the other hand was known more as a no-brainer. He kept Kelele's company because they seemed to go for the same local brew and he was usually in agreement when gossiping about the elders of the tribe, who were not really their cup of tea. However he always appeared to delay whatever he did or planned to do but he did seem to have his heart in the right place. He didn't appear to have enemies but neither did he have any decent friends. He lived not far from us and was always invited to our home parties. Kelele lived on the other side of Mavoko and continued linking up with Kinyua because they had been to school together, in Mavoko. Kelele knew my father but didn't have the courage or the good sense to talk to Dad directly about his opinions or suggestions.

Dad never interfered in the trade deals or market transactions that some of the villagers were involved in. This was in the 60s and 70s when the Akamba were still doing business with other large Kenyan tribes like the Kikuyu® who dominated the Kenyan scene for many years. The Akamba were hunter-gatherers who moved to agriculture and then to barter, and did quite a roaring trade in cane beer, ivory, brass amulets, tools, weapons and cattle with other tribes and with the Arab tradesmen on the coast. Soon other items like basketry, pottery and medicinal plants got included in the trade. Their successful trading helped the tribe to move towards the coast when the rains were poor for their crops further inland. It was a matter of time before some of these traders set up deals that gradually brought in an element of trickery and foul play, especially when there weren't many goods to trade with. There also seems to have been a hint at a slow drug trade that began creeping in during those times.

Dad never approved some of these deals and this was probably one of the reasons why Kelele did not see eye to eye with him. My Dad's deals and transactions were all above board as honesty for him was indeed the best policy! My mother was also a teacher in the local Junior School and both, Dad and Mum, had learnt to absorb the changes of developing times and of scientific progress in quite an analytical way. They were not held bound by traditional beliefs about what the birth of a child signified or about how they should bring up their children, or indeed about how they should live their lives. They were intelligent and well-informed and were able to make their own decisions.

The Akamba, for example, were particular about initiation rites, which were prerequisites for social

maturity. These rites, part of which had circumcision®
both for males and females, are a necessary part of
transformation of the individual within the social
structure. They take place at different stages from
infancy to adulthood. The tribal community believes
that it is their obligation to communicate their values,
their oral traditions and their way of life to their youth.
One of the learned scholars of the Akamba, John Mbiti
®, says that transitions, (e.g. the one that marks the end
of babyhood or childhood), offer a rite of separation
from one status to another and initiate individuals to the
rights and privileges of society, (e.g. to get married and
bear children, to fight for one's country, or to own
property). Probably because they held reasonably high
positions in a modern developing society Mum and
Dad did not feel obliged to conform in many of these
practices. As committed Christian believers they might
have felt that these did not seem appropriate to a
modern Christian or a Catholic way of life.

When I was born, the first girl after four boys, the
traditional-thinking villagers thought some sort of a
spell had been broken and that the 'gods' of our tribe
would now bring wealth, prosperity and importance to
the family, and to the clan. Some thought that this birth
would make us move back to tribal ways. Others
expected and hoped that especially Mum would get
more involved in the cultural traditions of the village
some of which had a lot to do with tribal functions that
may have bordered on forms of witchcraft perhaps.
That of course didn't happen, as both my parents were
staunchly Catholic and Christian in their outlook as
well as in the practices they adopted.

For the Akamba the birth 'rite-of-passage'®
introduces the baby into the community. The rite begins

with conception and ends with the actual birth, with the cutting of the umbilical cord. Both these events become integral parts of this extended rite. In fact, as happened in my case too in later life, pregnancy even if unplanned is always considered to be a treasured blessing, even if not openly spoken of. However, the birth of a child brings on the dual responsibility of protecting the vulnerable child from evil spirits and from certain people who have the evil eye®, and of naming the child. The child is therefore kept secluded until the naming ceremony. The naming ritual then transforms the newly born from the status of "it" to the status of a person. It is a big occasion when the name gives the child new life. The climax is when the name is officially pronounced, usually by the (paternal) grandmother (sometimes by the mother in some African groups e.g. in Nigeria), and the father puts a bracelet around the neck of the child. At this point all the women present ululate (*kusiilila*), which is the way the Akamba, (and other African groups), offer congratulations at major events. I was not put through all this I was told.

As I look back now I think that my parents were also quite modern for the times they lived in, and reasonably open and generous in the way they brought us up. Moreover we weren't really well-to-do but we weren't also down-and-out. We more than got by I'd say. We dressed alright and I do remember neighbours coming by to see what gifts or clothes we got for our birthdays or other celebrations. In fact as the first girl, after four boys in the family, everyone around us kept noticing anything and everything that I did. They wanted to know where my parents did their shopping to make me look so smart always.

Shopping? We weren't rolling in money but I was quite choosy about the little girlish things I wanted from a very young age. I saw children from better off families at school flash their expensive pens or their showy watches. The mobile phone wasn't yet around, but gold earrings and engraved bangles were, and so were trendy hair-styles. I couldn't keep up with all this or rather Mum couldn't afford it all. Yet if I did pick up something new to wear and wore it to school or even on visits to friends, it became the talk of the village.

I was the joy of my mother and the pride of my father, and they made sure that no one had anything untoward to say about me. They were just proud that I was their daughter, a well-behaved and properly turned-out girl brought up in the best traditions of the church and of the Akamba. They also did their best to groom me and to make me look like a little princess, well into my teens. Yet my mother couldn't help but continue to show her motherly concern, or was it a sort of control?

'Now, Annie, go and change that frock of yours,' she once said, when I was just six.

'I like it, Mum,' I remember saying.

'Yes, but dear,' she insisted, 'it's not good enough for Church. The Lord might not object, but some of our friends would.'

'Why? What's wrong with it?' I almost dared to ask, something I seldom did when my mother had an opinion or a piece of advice that seemed reasonable. It is also one of the traditions of the Akamba that children should never question their parents, especially their mothers. Children were made to respect the opinions of their parents and of their elders.

'There's nothing wrong with it, dear. It's just that the colours are too loud and showy for church. Wear it for a party or when we go visiting friends. Always check that your dress goes over your knees. Perhaps, for today...... wear that white and grey dress to church.'

It wasn't till I was about seven perhaps, that I began to realize what was happening around me. I seemed to be enjoying life, with everyone pampering me. I was actually fifth in a large family of 10: 5 boys and 5 girls. I was the only girl after the first 4 boys in the family, and that naturally brought great joy to the family, and quite obviously I became the pampered one. That isn't necessarily the way the birth of a girl is received in many African settings, and definitely not among the Akamba. The arrival of boy, not a girl, is the cause for celebration usually.

My parents had a staunch Christian outlook to life and a firm Catholic belief in principles. Christianity was first brought to Kenya by the Portuguese, in the fifteenth century, which was more the Catholic version than the Protestant® one, but the Protestants had more of an initial influence on the people as they came in numbers and in different groups or denominations that offered a variety of religious programmes. They also perhaps had a lot more backup with personnel, money and equipment. The earlier ones were the Presbyterians®, the Methodists, the Lutherans® and the Pentecostals®. They generally had American or British backgrounds and seemed better organized for their objectives. The Catholic educators and social workers usually came from Belgium, France, Italy and Spain which in those days, it would seem, did not really have the best bank balances in the world.

The Protestants were nearly 58% of the population with the Catholics only around 23%. Yet, somehow, in Africa, all these different groups were united in their benevolent and philanthropic approach to society especially in matters of education, health and social policies. The real differences only showed in their forms of worship and in their liturgy®. This Christian influence was noticeable not just in education and social work but as time went by many of the African political and social leaders were either practising Christians or because of their exposure to a broader and more 'open' education were able to appreciate the changing trends of modern society. So even if they did not become Christian they became more tolerant of views, practices and values different from their own.

Chapter 2: A time to keep : Looking back

The history of our family really starts with our grandparents, and dates back to the times when the colonial rulers, the British, were really ending their rule of Kenya (in the early 60s), and when our ancestors began taking over the reins of government and organization. My grandparents, especially as Akamba, weren't really directly involved, but they were part of that society that determined who we are today.

My mother's father was called Mwau. He was born near Nyeri, which is about 300 km north-east of Nairobi, Kenya's capital. The oral stories of the day, which sometimes are the only history that is passed on, record how he, when still a little boy, got separated from his family during a tribal raid. We do not really have a cohesive account of those days from Mwau as he was too young to remember any details, even when we tried to press him for details. These inter-tribal raids had to do with grabbing cattle or other possessions, or perhaps young male workers who could provide labour in farms or perhaps serve as back-up defenders in inter-tribal fights or skirmishes.

In the case of Mwau, there is a sort of distant resemblance to the story of Joseph® in the Bible, though Mwau was not sold by his brothers/relatives. Like him the raiders brought Mwau to Mavoko, a bigger trading point, over 200 km away, where they might have got a better deal. There isn't enough evidence to show whether he was sold or just given over to an Akamba family. The oral gossip handed down from local pub owners, who generally knew everyone passing by, said that he settled into the routine of his new family either because things were going smoothly or because he genuinely liked his new family. Whatever the facts were, this was really the beginning of the history of our family.

There in Mavoko he was raised by this family that followed traditional tribal ways. At this point it seemed clear that Mwau was not yet a baptised® Christian but we do not know whether he followed any tribal or traditional customs. It would appear that the exciting events in those days for young men were riding donkeys, poaching cattle and raiding farms. It was the order of the day. Wealth in fact was measured in terms of cattle and possessions, no matter how these were acquired. It was almost the philosophy of 'all is fair in love and raids'. In fact it was not unheard of, though not common, for macho raiders occasionally to carry off attractive girls or indeed young women. Yet our Mwau was in a class of his own, a sober and respected person busy with his own family. However, Mwau was apparently also employed by the colonialists and appears to have done some caretaker jobs on their farms and enterprises.

He must have excelled in his dutifulness and his industry because he was allowed to go to village school facilities, usually provided by the colonialists, where adults too had the option of some formal education. He probably did the equivalent of Standard 4 or perhaps more. We know that because he even taught my grandma to read and write both in Kikamba and in Kiswahili, the coastal language. Unfortunately he passed away when Mum was only 15. He got a bad attack of asthma and that took him to his grave when he was not very old really, probably in his early 70s.

Mum's mother, Felista, grew up in this Akamba traditional family with my grandfather of course. She was quite smart and had an excellent memory. I got to see her and to chat with her when I was doing Primary School. It is a pity that I didn't get her to talk more about those memorable early days. She didn't live very close to us, and the modern-day preoccupation with homework and tasks did not allow me to visit her as often as I might have liked to. Maybe I should have done that 2-hour walk oftener to her little traditional house and her small plantations where they grew maize, fruits and vegetables. What is perhaps interesting and important is that she told me on one of those occasions that they used to consult the only doctors known those days, tribal healers. They were also known as 'witch doctors' who practised healing, divining or other magical (or unexplainable) procedures that would seem to have made them acceptable as part of a tribal community. There weren't any serious decisions taken after these consultations but my grandma remembered that the occasional so-called doctor did pass by and offer advice.

'I was very scared,' she told me once, 'when my body began to ache. I had terrible fever for about a week.'

'What did you do?' I was curious to know. 'Did you call the doctor?'

'Doctor? We had no doctors. We only had what we called tribal healers or witch doctors.'

'Were they good? Did they help you?' I asked.

'Not really. But we had no choice. They used to say strange mumbling prayers, light a fire and then walk around us in a circle. Sometimes they touched us with some strange-looking potions which they put on our heads.'

'What happened then? Did you feel better?'

'I don't really know or remember....Sometimes I got better, sometimes nothing happened. Many of the people around us, and a few of our friends too, believed in these peculiar practices. So I had no choice. I had to agree to submit to them. Our families didn't really have much of a say.'

'So, how did you get better?'

'Now when I look back, I think it was probably malaria quite often. Malaria is one of those sicknesses that really gets a hold of your brain. You feel dazed, stupid and in some ways seem to hallucinate. In those days we didn't understand that. Those so-called doctors made us drink some bitter stuff. It was probably a herbal mixture, which is quite possibly what quinine offers today.'

'Did these medicines work?'

'Sometimes they worked, and at other times nothing happened. We were just made to believe that we would get better. We even had to pretend we felt better. Maybe the adrenalin inside us made us feel better. Or maybe just staying indoors, keeping warm and sticking to a plain diet helped.'

'Did you get this fever quite often?'

'Well, yes. About 3 or 4 times a year.'

'Did you have to call these doctors every time?' I wanted to know.

'I tried not to. We had to pay them good money, or give them a goat or a calf. It was expensive, and I really couldn't afford it.'

My grandma got married to my grandpa, Mwau, when she was around 20 in an Akamba traditional marriage ceremony. She is not too sure of how she became a Catholic but she does speak of the children, including my mother, going to school and meeting priests and then of the priests coming over to the house. At some point in time, when grandfather, Mwau, was still alive they became Catholics, and good ones too. Whatever they did they did with conviction and belief. Maybe that gene was effectively handed down to me. They were active in the Catholic Church, but I do not know if she and my grandfather got re-married in the Church. Even Mum does not seem to remember if that happened. My grandmother is still alive and must be around 100 years old now.

My father's father, known as Musili (meaning Judge), lived not far from the Mavoko area. He had just one brother, Ngumbau (meaning the brave one). He didn't have sisters. He became a Christian at a very young age. The family were farmers, and that's where life began for him. He was however a modern farmer, depending on coffee for cash. He had a large farm where he used to grow sugarcane and food crops like maize, beans, yams, arrow roots (also known as cocoa yams), peas, egg plants and capsicum. He also had an orchard that had oranges, grape fruit, plums, peaches and guavas. I remember going over to his farm with the family to enjoy the harvest feasts he used to organize for us all. He was very close to the family and everyone in the clan liked him.

Grandpa was a great guy, and I think he was quite fond of me. I still miss him. He was also the village advocate (quite what his name signified), who arbitrated when things were not going right in families. He could truly spin yarns and never ran out of advice and stories. He was a devout Christian and a church elder till he retired in the 80s. The early Christian priests had taught him to read and write so he spent most evenings reading his Bible. That is one clear memory I have of him. On Sunday afternoons at around sunset, seated on a cane chair in the courtyard, he would read the Bible. If we children were visiting, he would sit us around his chair and get us to listen to his readings.

Apart from being a Christian senior, Grandpa was also a village elder and spent part of his time adjudicating in matters that concerned the whole community. He was a respected member of our clan. He died at the age of 105. Asthma is what killed him as well. Didn't he do well to get to that age? Grandma was Mumbe (meaning beautiful). Apparently she was quite cute and pretty when she was born, and hence the name. She was also a truly humble person. She helped on the farm, and was a devoted housewife, the mother of 5 children (2 daughters, 3 sons).

She was converted to Christianity when she was a little girl. That brought a little coldness in her family relationships because her father was a traditionalist tribal leader. She was a convert of the first protestant priests – who founded the African Inland Church. My grandparents were exemplary Christians and maybe that deep sense (or gene perhaps) of Christian belonging was passed down to me. Mumbe lived to the ripe old age of 110.

My maternal grandma was a Catholic, but my paternal grandparents were staunch Protestants, so how did I end up being a catholic? Mum was raised a staunch Catholic. Dad was a teacher and when they were dating she made him agree to change to Catholicism as a condition for marriage. So really we are the only Catholic family in our immediate clan. I am proud to be Catholic. There is so much content and teaching in our beliefs that I feel sustained and supported in my living.

Dad and Mum as teachers got to know more about these differences among the various Protestant churches. My father was an intelligent man, very professional about his work and very dedicated to his clientele. As I grew up I began to understand the beliefs of the various Christian faiths. My parents however were exemplary and devout and were very clear about their Catholic views and teachings. I couldn't but imbibe these intensely tested traditions as they got handed down to me. My parents were probably in the league of second generation Catholics who had crossed that threshold of rites and symbolisms to genuine Christian beliefs and practices. As Catholics we were moving forward towards holier ways of living in the Catholic Church.

In fact, as I was growing up in my teens we had a very holy person around as the Catholic Archbishop of Nairobi, Cardinal® Otunga. People revered him as a person who had lived a life of exceptional sanctity in his lifetime. Mum closely followed his saintly life. He is now a Servant of God®, which is the first title given to a person on the way to being proclaimed a Saint in the Catholic Church. These Christian settings were strong incentives to get my parents urging me on towards a holy life in the Catholic Church. When Mum got pregnant with me, she later revealed to me one quiet evening, she had gone to one of the services conducted by the holy Cardinal so that she could receive his blessing. She prayed that his blessing might enable her to have a baby-girl. She had had four boys and was really longing for a girl. Dad too wanted a girl and of course my brothers couldn't but hope they'd get a baby sister. There was nothing really Akamba or African about that, where only the birth of a boy really matters. Whatever it was I turned up, and kind of turned everything around! It was almost quite like Cinderella® goes to the ball, or like some Princess Royale was born!

When a woman gets pregnant in almost any African country it always brings hope to the tribe, to the family and to the relatives. However the elders especially hope that pregnant mothers will deliver boys. The coming of a girl is precious only in as much as she will in time help in the process of procreation, which is also very important for every tribe. Every child born however is always believed to be a gift from God, in nearly all African traditions, and so a girl too is a blessing. However, my parents had crossed the threshold of those prognoses many moons back. My parents were pious Christians and just prayed fervently for a girl, in not quite the African mode. So, my birth was indeed greeted with unbounded joy and wild expectation in the inner circles of relatives and of the clan. I was perhaps too young to understand what all the fuss was about, but with four elder brothers and a doting Mum and Dad I was probably having the time of my life during those early years of mine. Pity there weren't any videos or digital cameras recording events else there might have been some nostalgic memories to relish today.

What didn't really sink in was that Mum was determined, as a committed Christian, from the time she weaned me, to bring me up as a model Christian girl, and hence her insistence on what I wore to church. She flooded me with pictures and stories of great

Christian saints like Maria Goretti®, Lucy®, Agnes®, Therese of Lisieux® and Joan of Arc®. She had these and other saints' pictures all over my room, and all over the house, besides of course pictures of the Last Supper®, the Holy Family®, Our Lady of Lourdes® or Saint Anthony® perhaps. I can't quite remember that gallery of saints.

Chapter 3: A time to laugh: The Joys of Family

We didn't live in a flashy or spacious home. It was a cottage-type of a house, with just 4 rooms: one for the boys and one for me and my parents apart from the sitting room and the dining-cum-kitchen. We were a little squashed perhaps but really had more than most families could afford in those days. There weren't cats or dogs as pets to occupy us, or indeed television to distract us. The internet hadn't come in yet. There weren't too many children of my age around. Mum's friends were regular church-goers and god-fearing people. As the only girl in the earlier half of the family I was Mum's 'tag along', to wherever she went, as her little pet as well as her proud 'promotional' treasure. That was of course until my younger sisters were born when I graduated from the sort of 'central' role to a more 'adult female' role of 'co-carer' of baby-females!

Going to church every Sunday was quite an event. We all made sure we presented ourselves as worthy children of our respected parents, as much for them as for the Lord in Church. We went through that chore each week as a sort of completion of all our other social obligations, e.g. going to school, going to meet friends, or going to other public or not-so-public functions. We had to dress neatly and smartly and had to take up the front seats in church and get involved in some parts of the liturgy of the Mass like the offertory® procession or, later when we grew up, in doing the readings. Everyone in the village would notice this with some even believing that we were trying to put on a show. It wasn't like that at all. We did it as part of our upbringing. It all became spontaneous for us. There was no arrogance or display about it either. We actually felt thrilled to be part of the Church.

My Dad was quite a respected person as a teacher and Head-teacher. He didn't just feel proud of me, he quite adored me. My four elder brothers who protected me loved me to bits. As my other brothers and sisters began to come along I began to take on some of the mothering roles of Mum. This often happens in some African tribes where parents space out the births of their children so that the elder ones can step in to baby-sit the younger ones. Each time a new member was added to the family I got additional roles especially as the senior-most female in the family. As time went by I noticed that my opinions too began to be respected a lot more as I tended to stay at home. This changed a little when later I went to boarding school and my brothers (and later on my sisters) took on more responsible roles, as they moved on in their studies or in their careers.

In fact my brothers particularly went into challenging careers. My eldest brother, Alwyn, became a financial consultant, my second brother, Athyn, a social worker, my third, Agstyn, a curio dealer and my fourth, Antyn, a senior accountant. My other brother, Andryn became an agricultural expert. My sister, just younger to me, Adreya, became an Education adviser, while my other sisters Agnesa, Agatha and Anesa took on respectable professions. My sisters' names started in an 'a' and ended with an 'a': all three-syllable names. My brothers' names also started in an 'a' but all ended in a 'yn': only two-syllable names. I must certainly have meant something special to my parents after they had had four boys. Probably that's why my name was different, a longer name than everyone else, and unlike all the others, a five-syllable name, yet starting and ending with an 'a': Anastasia, sort of ensuring I was part of the family.

My Mum had something to do with the girls' names, possibly her love for Italian-sounding names. This may have been some influence she had from two Italian volunteer-worker families who were involved in agricultural projects in our area, who became friends of our family. My Dad did some work for a Dutch farmer and had a Danish friend who ran a financial consultancy, and so thought he'd give some European-sounding names to the boys. Yet both my parents agreed that all our names would begin with an 'a'. We were such a large family that we were quite a community by ourselves. In fact we didn't miss people so much as we made up quite a number when it came to birthdays and parties. We boys and girls were always close to each other and had enough to talk about or to do within our household that we perhaps had little time for others, for friends. My real friendships began only when I started school.

Our local Junior School was only a ten-minute walk away, and as we walked to school other children from the houses around would join us and we soon became a merry band often humming or singing as we trotted off to school. I found learning easy and fascinating. It wasn't long before I became a star in my class and then in my school. I didn't find any subject particularly difficult and was quite an inquisitive child. The teachers seemed to like that. Soon I was also in the school singing group and on festive occasions took part in the little plays, as did some of my siblings. I do remember playing the lead role in the African versions of Goldilocks and of Red Riding Hood. I also began to win prizes in school competitions and my parents' joys knew no bounds. They also noticed that I was hungry for knowledge and that the local school wasn't perhaps stretching my intelligence or my talents. They also felt that I needed more constant care even at school as they saw me maturing as a teenager. They started building plans for me. Perhaps the seeds of change in my life were sown during this 'good season' in my life.

There was a spark of faith and sharing that Mum had implanted in me, and Dad's sterling example had infused a sense of dignity and fairness that seemed to have left an imprint on me. I also felt that because we were honest people we deserved fair treatment no matter what we did. I started to get annoyed when I didn't get things going the way I wanted them to be. It began when I didn't do as well as I was expected to do. I missed out winning in some competitions at school and that annoyed me. The God-reliance infused into me by my parents, especially Mum, began to get tested.

I know I once came back from school in tears. It was as if my world had collapsed. It was a bit of a storm in a teacup. No, I hadn't lost the war. I'd just lost a minor battle. I came 2nd in a singing contest. Not the end of the world, but for me it was. I just couldn't take it. So I began new battles, a series of quarrels with the Lord that were to last all my life.

'Why did You let her win?' I complained to Him. 'You knew I was better. I tried so hard, and yet You let her win. I'm really angry with You.'

That spontaneous childish candour has probably never left me. That defeat at age six was hard to swallow, as I look back on it now. I soon got over it as I began to win other contests. To add to this my brothers pampered me all the time and cheered me up through unpleasant or difficult times. Did I say 'difficult'? Nothing was really difficult. I think I was spoiled, totally. It was as if the world was my oyster. I was Dad's pet and Mum's girl. Mum was aware about the situation around us, about the number of broken homes, of unwanted pregnancies and of teenage girls almost running riot. In fact there were, and probably still are, hundreds of teenage pregnancies to cope with each day in Kenya. She kept reminding me to read the lives of Maria Goretti, Therese of Lisieux and other female model Saints like Lucy, Agnes, Bernadette® and Joan of Arc. I was, I felt, protected from any weakening influence on my life or personality. Mum really kept a close eye on me and I just drank it all in. I didn't question her wisdom and did my best to be her good girl.

Mum and Dad also drew on the traditions of the great Akamba people. 'Remember, you are an Akamba,' they kept saying. Perhaps not a day went by without Dad especially reminding me of the great leaders of our tribe, even though I didn't take on, even as a second name, a name of one of my ancestors, or that of a great Akamba, which is the custom. I could have had a second name like Stella [Stella Kilongo –a leading business person] or Charity [Charity Kaluki Ngilu – a prominent politician] added to my name.

Though my parents were proud to be Akamba they did not want to go through all the Akamba traditions like initiation, child naming and rites of passage, as I mentioned earlier. Child Naming is a significant facet of the Akamba culture. Children are often lovingly called names like Musumbi which means (the 'king'), and Muthoki (which means 'long awaited one'). In most cases, children are named after events surrounding their birth. For instance, Nduku is given to a baby girl born at night and Mutuku to a baby boy born at night.

My parents, besides not really being taken in by all these cultural trends, wanted me just baptised as a Christian in church and with the usual Christian liturgy. They later held a short baptism/christening party to which they invited their neighbours, some Christian and non-Christian folk. Later, because the neighbours insisted and because I was the first girl in the family (and one of very few girls in the clan), my parents agreed to a small cultural function at a community venue to which they invited many more elders of the village and some local dignitaries. These elders just loved their solemn roles and came up proudly and blessed me. Some of the elderly women also got together to sing a traditional chant where my name was mentioned. The younger ones celebrated with dances and songs. I was of course in cloud baby-land totally oblivious to all the fuss going on around me. Mum told me, years later, that I merited a certificate of 'good baby conduct', as I didn't cry, made efforts to smile, and did not object to the elders' fussing over me, which of course enhanced her position in the clan.

My parents chose to ignore the culturally loaded involvement of the naming rite and went for a simpler ceremony where Mum decided to call me by a rather uncommon name, a name longer than any of my siblings, 'Anastasia'. Not sure why my parents chose the name for me, but probably it was Mum who was chiefly responsible. Anastasia was a 5th century Catholic saint, of Roman descent, who was martyred during the Christian persecution under the Roman

Emperor Diocletian®. She has the rare distinction of being mentioned in the Canon® of the Mass®, the most important and sacred part of this main Catholic liturgy. She was invoked as the patron saint for healers and exorcists. It is believed that her relics can still be traced to a church in present-day Croatia, though there is also in present-day Istanbul (formerly Constantinople) a church dedicated to her. She is also the patroness of widows and of those who suffer from poisons or the effects of harmful substances.

By a strange coincidence (I'm not sure Mum was aware of this) Saint Anastasia, as recorded in the Synaxaria® (or recorded lives of holy people in the middle ages) was born of a non-Christian (pagan) father, Prepextatus, and Fausta, a Christian mother. Her mother too later became a Saint, and was associated with the great teacher Saint Chrysogonus®. There is no evidence to show that her distinguished Roman father converted to Christianity but her family was very pious and followed Christian traditions. She grew up to spend her life as an exemplary Christian. So it would seem appropriate that this was probably the ideal name chosen by Mum to unite the Christian and non-Christian (Akamba) traditions. I think this is what may have struck my mother and this is what she wanted me to be: a very good Christian, leading a life of true piety, purity and service, as well as an outstanding Akamba, standing up for the best non-Christian traditions.

I hadn't researched the background of my saint until quite recently, and feel awed by the greatness of the Saint as well as by the holy pressures and expectations it puts on me, even today as an adult, to live up to them. My friends still try to cope with this five-syllable name. 'A-nas-ta-si-a' is quite a mouthful of a name, and my brothers and sisters find it easier to call me either 'Ansy' or just 'Anas'. My youngest brother still calls me just 'Ana', which seems to be the name that stuck with some of my peers through my school days and even with my mates in later years. Most of those who know me today call me just 'Ana', which when anglicized sounds more like 'Anna' or just Ann.

We lived in the Mavoko area, not more than 200 km away from the outskirts and south east of Nairobi. In fact, though our tribe, the Akamba, moved to Kenya originally from the western parts of Tanzania, the country to the south of Kenya, in East Africa, we were in the heartland of the tribe, which is broadly in the Mavoko area. So, while our parents and my brothers took active interest in all that happened around us, including the festivities of our neighbours, they kept a socially acceptable distance from functions that didn't seem to be above board in their view. Some of these celebrations went on for weeks and would involve the sharing or offering of gifts that may have included goats or cattle in the common celebrations.

Yet my parents, probably because Dad was quite knowledgeable as a teacher, didn't really get involved in the initiation rites of some of our neighbours nor in the somewhat clandestine female circumcision occasions, though nearly all these traditions had almost died out by the time I was born. I think that either out of pressure, or for the sake of goodwill, my parents might have contributed a chicken or a kid for a celebration or a function. In a way they probably didn't even want me to know more about these traditions that may have been around as I was growing up.

Soon the real tests of my life would begin. My parents felt that the only way to take me out of the not-very-agreeable aspects of the local influences was to get me away from Mavoko. They also felt I needed to get a sound education which they would not be able to provide for at home. This was not available in the local schools around, though they were good and comprehensive in their own right. There were no Catholic or Christian priests or nuns who ran schools close to Mavoko in those days. So, they sent me away to boarding school to Meru, in north east Kenya, nearly 300 km away from Mavoko, i.e. away from where our grand-parents had settled down a long time back. I spent four wonderful and exciting years in the boarding school in Meru that left lasting impressions on me. In many ways they laid solid foundations for me both in learning academic work as well as in developing my personality. I think the 'building' that is Anastasia today had its framework built in the boarding school in Meru.

The school was run by the Sisters of Mercy, an Order founded by the Comboni Fathers but managed by the Consolata Fathers, both Orders dedicated to serving the people. Both these Orders were pioneers in education and social work not just in Kenya but in several other parts of Africa too. The Sisters of Mercy had the true spirit of Daniel Comboni, (the Italian priest from Verona in Italy, who founded these Orders for men and for women). They looked after all our needs and our development. The Consolata Fathers, who managed the school, now work in 20 countries around the world doing immense good to people through their education, health care and social plans.

I think I imbibed this great 'Catholic' (or 'universal') spirit of generosity and warmth that the Sisters seemed to exude. In fact I liked the Sisters so much that I hoped I could one day be like one of them and serve others. In my prayers I know I kept saying, 'Lord look after me, and prepare me to become one of them, when I grow up.'

Yet in those early years of fervour I seemed to get no feedback from my great Lord. There seemed to be a feeble voice telling me, 'I don't think you're meant to be one of them.' I wasn't sure then of what that message signified. Maybe it had to do with their strict life, or their longish habits. Yet I liked that brown long robe and the way that it combined with the white bib-like top. The Sister-in-Charge, Sister Philomena, who was from Italy, was like my Mum: so caring and loving. I could go to her for anything I needed or whenever I felt a bit uncomfortable, as when I had my troublesome periods. I know I got my peers to explain it all to me, but she was there to listen to me when I got irritable or unwell. She encouraged me to keep up my childish trust in the Lord.

I know that in spite of that protection and care I still kept complaining to the Lord constantly. 'Why do women have to go through all this?' I asked. 'You know the pain and awkwardness I have to go through. Don't You understand? I miss all the fun the other girls are having. Can't You give me some relief? Can't You let it roll on a bit faster just suppose I can't avoid it?'

Of course there was no answer, and I had to take it on my chin. My mother had prepared me for all this before I went to school, and kept checking on me when I returned home for my holidays, and so I knew it was all coming. Yet it was difficult to take as I was a sort of an enthusiast, almost wanting to jump out of my skin just to be in everything. My periods left me quite weak and inactive though my mind was as alive as ever. My

46

little clique of friends supported me through my difficult days and was constantly around me, picking my brains, asking for ideas and planning ahead. So, somehow I still felt I was in control even if out of action.

Yet there were times I wanted to get help from doctors or 'medicine men'. Some of my mates called them tribal healers, while others referred to them as 'witch doctors'. I also remembered some of those stories of my grandmother, though I know now that all these had little to do with any witchcraft. I had depressing times, moments of feeling low, e.g. during my periods. My peers would also talk about these experiences of their parents, relatives or elders, and of how these doctors sometimes got them out of bad times or at other times were just part of the goings-on of tribal life.

It is interesting to note that a survey conducted in 2010 by the Pew Research Centre, a US-based organisation dealing in religious research showed that a quarter of Kenyans believe in witch doctors even though they are deeply religious. However in spite of impressive religious credentials, strong belief in the existence of one God, heaven and hell, the survey found that sub-Saharan Africa, Kenya included, leads in the worship of alternative gods -- witchcraft, evil spirits, and sacrifices to ancestors, traditional religious healers and reincarnation.

A quarter of Kenyans, Christians included, confessed they believed in the protective power of juju (charms or amulets) and that they consult traditional healers. A number admitted to revering their dead ancestors and treasuring animal skins and skulls or knowing of friends or relatives who identify with these faiths. With all this common talk around me I couldn't but be led on to believe that perhaps I might well have tried out some of this, in spite of my strong Catholic upbringing. I now thank heaven I didn't.

Sickness is a very common problem faced in Akamba-land. Malaria, pneumonia, colds, and coughs, worm diseases, stomach ailments, eye diseases, body sores, tuberculosis and women's ailments are among the most prevalent. Diseases are often attributed to the power of black magic®. Akamba doctors are known as 'andu-awe' (medicine-men, or herbalists). They prescribe cures for many of the diseases that are common among the Akamba using herbs and roots, and sometimes charms and rituals. Such doctors are highly respected, or are perhaps the only 'knowledgeable' folk around. People go to them for consultations of every type, though as far as I am aware my family didn't use them. Some of my brothers in later years would appear to have had contact with them, but my parents didn't get involved and did warn us about them, even though they did not really explore these connections or involvements to be able to tell us more. These practices are really different from what specialists in African Studies call witchcraft.

These doctors' professions have been overshadowed but not altogether replaced by western-trained doctors and nurses. The recorded incidents and the stories circulating seem to suggest that 'herbal doctors' perform valuable services for local communities by treating the sick, counteracting the power of witchcraft, and providing people with possible solutions and some cures. In some cases they have proved to be a support or a refuge especially in shielding or healing people suffering from the after-effects of witchcraft particularly. Their combined physical and psychological approach to sickness and suffering could well provide a support to some aspects of medical work in Africa. In my desperation at school, especially because I was away from the loving care of Mum, I wanted some of these herbs or remedies to heal me, or at least relieve my pains. I wasn't looking for witchcraft. I wanted just plain relief from whatever was available, and I didn't bother about what it was called. I am glad I didn't go down that route.

However in spite of these apparent hiccups, and my dabbling in knowledge of these not-very-reputable remedies, I shone in school at all the activities: dancing, drama, sports, quizzes and home-science projects. Mum and Dad were on top of the world with all the reports I sent them of my progress at school. They might have had my name up on billboards, if they could, for they were truly thrilled with the performance of their 'Girl'! I couldn't wait to go home for my vacations, and yet I loved school and just longed to get back to my stardom in school after each holiday. Back home of course I was the pride of my parents. Mum was delighted with my growing up so successfully in boarding school. Both my parents were pleased that they had done the right thing for me. They always did their best to present me as the model girl of the village.

The four years at boarding helped me to mature as a girl, and I was the little 'queen' for my brothers, who were so proud of me. Yet, I didn't get on to other male friends, or boyfriends for that matter. My passion for everything that bordered on Church or religious living almost enraptured me and in a way propelled me to an imaginary fantasy of life in the future. I wanted to grow up in a hurry and save the world and become a champion of goodness and charity. I had models in front of me like Mother Theresa of Calcutta®, Teresa of Avila, Joan of Arc and of course my own namesake, Saint Anastasia®. My puberty years had almost swept by me with hardly a trace of longings or harsh realities that other teenagers seem to go through. Those cravings for herbal remedies were just temporary blips. I recovered very quickly from the dumps and was up and about faster than most other girls. I wanted to move fast-forward. I just wanted to join an Order and get on with life. I had in a way fallen in love with the Lord and indeed with all the activities of the Church, especially with the work of the nuns who were educating me.

Chapter 4: A time to build: The joys of living

When I was in Form 3 (the equivalent of Standard 9), also my 3rd year in Senior School, and I was around 14, I began to feel this renewed interest in nuns. For me the nuns were like angels. I liked the way they swished about in their habits, smiling around, offering advice, helping us through our chores, our studies and resolving our petty quarrels. They were wonderful counsellors to me even though perhaps they still kept a sort of aloofness from us. They mixed with us during the breaks in our academic work or chores or at other interval times when we were in a more relaxed mode, sharing in some of our conversations or perhaps our jokes. Yet there was a certain distance that was maintained, probably more by us than by them. Typical of teenage girls, we didn't want to let them into our 'real' secrets! Maybe they too felt they might intrude into our childish or teenage crazy conversations, or perhaps that we might laugh at their ignorance on matters teenage, girlish or trivial. But they were always there, always available and always helpful. That left a mark on me. This feeling within me of wanting to be like them began to grow on me.

Naturally we girls had our favourites, among the nuns I mean. I liked all of them, but there was one I particularly liked, Sister Sabine, maybe because she was the only one who seemed like us. She was from a mixed African background. She looked more African than European and still had traces of a bit of a French-African accent. Whenever I got a chance I used to throw little darts at her in the form of questions. More than just being an inquisitive child I was always eager to get to know things for myself. It was my subtle way of trying to find out more about her life and the life of the Sisters, if at some point in time I did indeed choose to be a nun. I didn't want the nuns to probe into my intentions. I had to play this low key even though this feeling was getting stronger all the time.

'Do you wear ordinary pyjamas or special night dresses when you go to bed, Sister?' I asked Sister Sabine one day.

She looked a bit embarrassed but did reply saying, 'Oh you little sweetie. We're ordinary. We wear what we like, and what's comfortable when we go to bed.'

Another time I asked her, 'Do you miss home? Do you enjoy your work?'

Sister Sabine, always the professional, didn't have a problem answering my silly questions. 'Well, in a way we miss home. It's pretty natural. But we're happy to be Sisters and to be doing our work. We do go home once every 2 years to visit our parents or relatives just to keep in touch, but we don't long for home. We've given up all that. You girls are our family now.'

It was the kind of thing I was waiting to hear but I still felt intrigued on how the nuns got on. I never seemed to spot them having a quarrel or a disagreement. Whenever one nun said something the other would agree. They never seemed to be at odds on any issues. I couldn't believe that. I had petty quarrels with my mates nearly every day, or perhaps a few times a day. I had a sneaky feeling Sister Sabine wasn't telling me all.

'Sister, don't you ever have a disagreement with another nun?' I felt bold to ask.

'Well, we do disagree at times, but we discuss things. We meet in community, or we go to our Sister Superior if we find it hard to agree, and that's how we sort out things, much the way you girls, I'm sure, come to agree on things. We're human....we just work out things.'

Then almost out of nowhere I had my first rude shock in life. Sister Sabine had guided me so well. She seemed to understand all my mood swings and gave me so much valuable information. She knew I was in a kind of dreamland wanting to give myself to God and knew of my desire to become a nun. She had given me several addresses of religious Orders to write to. I was funny and sometimes even discussed with her my fascination for particular types of dresses or habits® that the sisters wore. She would often laugh at my strange interests but never failed to encourage me. In fact I found the habits of the Contemplative® Orders of nuns more appealing and attractive than even the one that Sister Sabine was wearing. She was friendly and patient, and kept telling me that my choices would change as I grew older.

She was right. I soon got in touch with an Order that worked for the spread of the Gospel® message through direct involvement with people in parishes and with young people in institutions. I called them 'The Sisters of Christ'® (SOC). I felt I wanted to be a speaker and a promoter of God's Word, and I knew that their friendly, simple and ordinary way of life would suit me. I liked the way they conducted open seminars where people could express their views on the way the Gospel could be spread. It was different from hospital work or teaching in schools. I didn't like their habit but I liked the work they did. Sister Sabine even told me that

53

perhaps I should follow up that interest, which I did. Then one day, almost quite suddenly, I found Sister Sabine was not seen around in the convent for a quite a few days and then for a few weeks. I naturally grew a bit anxious. The other sisters told me she had gone off on some work to another convent. When she didn't return over the next few weeks I asked again. This time they told me she had been transferred. I soon realized that she wasn't coming back to this convent at least.

On my next trip home, some months later, after a bit of research, I found out that she had been told to leave. Eventually I traced her to the outskirts of the city of Nairobi. I was in tears at seeing her struggle in life, to start life all over again, but she seemed to smile and to take it in her stride. She had found a job, working in a clothing factory, just sewing garments in a production line. Yet it was a rude shock to me who was so eager to join an Order. What if the nuns I joined up treated me like that one day? I just couldn't understand why such a good and capable person had been asked to leave, and then to find her there, sort of dumped out of society into something so mechanical, not fulfilling the great potential in her, and not using the invaluable knowledge and the skills she had. She had been my role model, my adviser and even one I'd shared jokes with. She had helped me contact so many other religious Orders, often even drafting the letters for me. She seemed so realistic, so loving and so truly helpful. I struggled to come to terms with it all. It was perhaps my first rude awakening and I couldn't believe what I had seen. Somehow I ploughed on eager to follow my dream. I of course couldn't help but quarrel about this with the Lord.

'What have You done to her? She was my friend, my great helper. And how can You stay out there and see her suffer so much? She was for me my model, an ideal nun, and You have dumped her there in a factory? Don't You think You're going a little over the top? Can't You do something about it? She's a good person. I know she hasn't done anything wrong. Get her out of that job. I really want You to do something about it....Please, Lord!'

What was even stranger was that my friend Sabine, besides refusing to tell me why she had left or was asked to leave the Order, even advised me not to be shaken from my purpose seeing her leave, but to continue to pursue my dream. From bits of conversation we had it looked like she was probably asked to leave because they found out (at quite a late stage, and probably just by accident) that she was an illegitimate child. Illegitimate children in those days could not become religious or nuns. I couldn't understand then how illegitimacy could be a problem. I was aware even then that many children born in Africa, or for that matter in other parts of the world, are born illegitimate and do well in life. I later found nuns and priests who had come from illegitimate backgrounds. Sabine had Temporary Vows and could be asked to leave if problems arose, i.e. before she could be allowed to take Final Vows. Sabine never told me what had really happened to her. She only kept encouraging me. She felt sure I'd make a good nun whichever Order I joined. I told her that I had made up my mind to join the Sisters of Christ. She seemed pleased for me and told me I could call on her for any assistance she could offer.

Later on, when in my first year of Novitiate training, with the SOC Order, I had found a good friend in Sister Asha, a nun from India. She was one of those responsible for teaching us different academic subjects and was also on hand for some of our basic needs like getting items of stationery, toiletry or clothing. Besides being a good Maths and Science teacher she also had a caring side. She turned out to be a good listener and a sound adviser too. Many of us felt comfortable talking to her about our little problems. She seemed to be more approachable and found time to be with us unlike the other nuns who seemed to keep their distance for reasons best known to them. This behavioural trend of these other nuns didn't appeal to me very much. I knew that if I ever became a nun I'd stay close to my students and to those I worked for, more like Sister Asha.

Anyway, Sister Asha noticed me floundering a bit in some of my thinking and, during one of my chats with her, suggested I read a particular book to give me inspiration and food for thought. She advised me to read 'Life of the Beloved' by Henri Nouwen®. It was a sincere testimony of the power and invitation of Christ to live a truly uplifting spiritual life in today's world. The book totally fascinated me and gave me food for thought. It became my constant companion and I truly absorbed its powerful suggestions for real living.

In a way, even the negativity that came along later with the sudden disappearance of my other good friend, Sister Sabine, got tided over with messages from this precious book. I still read extracts from the book even today. It is a book I would recommend to anyone struggling with negative thinking or depression.

Chapter 5: A time to dance: Learning different steps

Finally the search was over. I packed my belongings and literally dived into this commitment I had been longing for all my life. I joined the Postulants® of the Sisters of Christ (SOC). My first year was like my honeymoon: no worries, no hassles, just plain sailing. I was that little trout swimming gleefully and crazily in the little pond, my small community. Sister in charge, Sister Antonia, from Spain, was more than a mother to me, attending to all my silly needs and helping me to build a life of prayer and commitment. If fact she spent a lot of time trying to nurture me, the restless person that I was, into becoming an ideal nun, a peaceful, prayerful and composed person. That must have helped because all the Sisters noticed this and were pleased with me and my progress. They even sent glowing reports home to Mum in whose opinion I had become her little Saint.

Then once again almost out of nowhere unexpected surprises popped up. In our second year of training we had to do some experience trials. We were sent out, in little groups of course, to the outlets of the Sisters of Christ, to places where they wanted their trainees to get to know how people in parishes respond to the Gospel message. At these 'encounters' (as they were called) they had some sales and distribution going on as well of pamphlets on the Gospel or on the lives of Saints. I was sent to one such encounter in a parish, in a slum area outside Nairobi. The parish® was run by the White Fathers, another great Catholic Order doing immense good in Africa, in schools, parishes, community projects and social initiatives. While at the encounter session I noticed a little boy, probably about 8 years of age, who was standing quite aimlessly near the entrance. He was poorly dressed and skinny, and seemed to be pleading with his eyes for some attention. There weren't many people attending the 'encounter' sessions that morning and there were others of my mates not too occupied who could cope with the clients who came in, so I decided to walk up to the little lad and ask him what he wanted.

When I went up to him I was shocked to see his poor condition: he didn't have decent clothes and he seemed to be poorly nourished and seemed to me to be really in need of attention. What he told me worried me even more. There I was in my neat and tidy postulant's dress bending over quite patronizingly wanting to show involvement in 'encounters' that now looked meaningless with the reality of the boy right beside me. Here was a little lad who wanted food and clothing, basic stuff, not empty talk or 'interaction' (as it was called). I felt like a sore contradiction. What was I trying to 'encounter' really? Shouldn't I perhaps have been doing something at least to relieve a little bit of poverty, and showing some care, maybe offering him some food?

'What do you want?' I asked him in as kind a way as I could speak.

'I want something to eat,' he replied.

'Don't you get any food at home?' was my not-so-very helpful tone.

'No,' he replied as he began to cry.

'Why doesn't your father try and help you?' I persisted in a rather patronizing way, assuming that all parents are bound to provide for their children.

'My father's drunk all day and does nothing for the family....' he spoke through his tears.

That hit me a bit, but I wanted to know more and asked, 'Do the priests here help you?'

'Yes....sometimes,' he mumbled through his tears.

As my eyes now started welling up I was almost afraid that his next question might possibly have been a request, 'Can you help me?'

I felt so helpless, with no money on me and nothing to give this little boy. The incident shocked me. I spent the rest of the encounter day sobbing intermittently and trying to come to terms with what my life would be in this Order that to me appeared to be out of touch with reality, as I saw things.

Back in the convent I did not have an appetite for supper that evening. The needs of the poor, the hungry and the destitute were eating into me. I was livid and somewhat restless. When later in the evening Sister in Charge of the Novices, Sister Joanna, asked us to share our experiences I was quite outspoken in trying to express my disappointment because I couldn't help that little boy. Sister Joanna wasn't impressed at all, and certainly wasn't interested in my story.

Sister was from Italy and most of the other sisters in charge of us were from France, Belgium or Spain. There were no African Sisters yet on their team of trainer Sisters and my favourite Spanish nun, Sister Antonia, who was like a mother and a guide to me on several occasions, was not around at this particular point. She had gone away to another institution for rest and medical care. There was one sister with a sort of an African background, but she was not purely African. She was half Belgian and she happened to be a good friend of Sister Joanna. For some reason she never seemed to show any empathy towards our needs. She appeared to us to be one who had crossed over to the 'foreigner' or European side, where preferences were concerned. I wasn't really comfortable talking to her.

When I look back now I realize that these well-intentioned Sisters, very much like the nuns in the film Sister Act®, probably didn't really appreciate the broader context of what happens outside their convents, in spite of their God-given mandate to promote the objectives of their Order. They were keen on getting the Order established in Kenya and in Africa, on their own sort of European agendas, actually not really considering what was good for Africa. Whether they made an effort to understand Africans and African culture and sensitivities or not I'm not sure but they seemed bent on doing whatever it took to implant the Order in Kenya. Without appearing to show any preferences, they felt that their policies were forward thinking, constructive and realistic enough to them. They didn't feel obliged to ask us for opinions, and definitely not for advice.

They knew that the Order would have to move forward in spite of the attendant poverty around. Poverty, they felt, was a reality that had to be handled differently and certainly not directly by their Order. That was a task for Governments and for others. That's exactly what Sister Joanna tried to put across to me and to my other mates. She even looked a bit surprised that I was so worked up at the plight of the little boy. She boldly told the group of us novices that if we could not contain our feelings we should perhaps join another Order, like Mother Teresa's Order perhaps, that looked after poor and abandoned young people, and that the SOC was not for them. In her final exhortation she even showed a bit of temper and came close to a warning that postulants who could not keep their feelings in check would not be able to absorb the true spirit of the training of the SOC Order.

Not long after that I had my second shock. Complications set in at another unexpected speed-breaker I failed to see. On a visit home for my usual break at the end of my first year of Novitiate I suddenly developed a crush on a priest. Maybe it was the fact that I found life at home too far removed from my novitiate life. Or perhaps I just wanted to feel more linked to something, or perhaps someone, working and thinking at a more 'religious' level. I didn't also realize that with so much free time on my hands and with no regular religious routine to tie me down my lazier self, my hormones, could take over and go into crazy mode.

The new priest in our church, a really nice guy, an African for a change, and someone my parents liked so much, began to frequent our home. Actually he just wanted to be of assistance to me and my mother during the few weeks I was around. It turned out however that each time he visited us, (and he was at our house every other day even if just for a few moments), I grew in my fondness for him. I really began to like the guy: a good sincere man, who preached lovely sermons® and who was quite a star with the people as well. He was so kind and gentle with the children and with the elderly folk. He knew how to spend ample listening to people's problems and also went around visiting homes, blessing the sick, comforting parents and seniors, and cheering up children.

He spent decent amounts of time at home and listened to me quite a lot, showing understanding and empathy always. In some ways I felt he was more like a buddy than a priest. I felt comfortable talking about things that perhaps I wouldn't talk about so freely even with Mum. I soon found myself getting close not just to his thinking and to his reasoning but to him as a person. I found him soft in his speech, gentle in his approach and wonderful as a man. Towards the end I found myself grabbing his hands to feel closer. Once we actually got a good hug, with no one at home sneaking in to see us together. I'm not sure how he took that, but I know I definitely went into over-drive, letting myself into a warm and long bear hug! Maybe he too was developing a soft spot for me, or more? Whatever it was, he somehow held himself well. I wasn't sure then if he too had let his feelings go when we hugged. I was too confused to ask him.

I couldn't believe that in the space of just three weeks, the length of our holiday, I was actually falling in love. This was really the first time I felt the woman inside me trying frantically to get released. I used to laugh at some of the secrets a few of the other Novices shared with me about the relationships they had got into before they joined. I couldn't believe such thoughts were now entering my mind. All that fervour of becoming a nun and of being dedicated seemed to have disappeared, at least temporarily.

In my sober moments I couldn't believe this change was taking place in me. I began to feel more like a woman, more like the feelings I had experienced soon after puberty came on. I guess it was the sort of emptiness I was feeling, a kind of depression caused possibly by Sister Joanna's blasts at me earlier. Whatever it was, I was in a state of confusion. I might normally have discussed this with my new priest friend, but how could I discuss my crush on him of all people?

So I had to get back to my only Listener. I started another quarrel.

'Why are You doing this to me? I thought I was above all this. You should really have been controlling me. Now my heart has run riot. I just cannot contain my sensual and sexual feelings as well. Can't You stop this happening to me, Lord? You know I still want to go on. I still want to be a nun. What do I do with these wild feelings for a man? Yes, it's the woman in me just oozing out. I am aware that I am developing more and more into a woman, but I didn't expect to go overboard. And to make it worse, he's a priest. I just hope he has not picked this up. It could spell disaster for him too. Guide me, please! Yes, this is an SOS message to You. I need a quick reply.' I prayed fervently. How I wish today I could have set up some sort of a telephone-link service with Him, with the Lord I mean.

Returning to the convent after the holiday was true relief. Was I trying to escape from something? Was I afraid to face reality? I'm not sure but by the time I returned to the convent, quite strangely, these amorous feelings had cooled off a lot. In fact they had actually almost disappeared. There was still the trace of a little cry some nights, perhaps a sort of longing for a good opportunity missed to explore my womanly feelings a bit more.

However soon overall control returned and the whole incident seemed to be fading away, with only some sort of a longing occasionally flashing up in the distance that I didn't find difficult to flush out. Maybe I had crossed that hurdle and my crush seemed to have gone. All the same I felt urged to mention this unusual turmoil to Sister Joanna. I thought long and hard about it and finally decided to play the sincerity card and bring it into the open rather than hide it. I wish my friend and adviser from Mavoko, Father Lucien, had been around. I was on my own, with no one to guide me, and had to steer my head and my heart in the right direction and get the right analysis across to Sister.

Chapter 6: A time to mend: Facing realities

Then there was a third shock. I was in my fourth year with the SOC Order. It was my second year of novitiate, one of the two vital years before joining an Order. It was six months into the year when the celebrations for Kenya's Independence Day, 12th December, one of the biggest days for Kenya, my homeland, came along. It was a huge celebration for Kenyans commemorating the day they got freedom from British rule. It was an annual public holiday when the whole country rejoiced and celebrated. It is true we were in a convent but we felt strongly that we also still belonged to our countries. At least this is what I thought. Of the 9 of us novices in the group two were from Madagascar, the large island country off Africa's east coast, and one was from South Africa. The rest of us were from Kenya.

When checking on our schedule for the day we found out it would be a normal day: study and work. There was nothing on the agenda even suggesting an extra prayer session for our country. This caused general unease amongst all of us novices. Everyone felt that someone had to make a move, perhaps at least to inform Sister in Charge, Sister Joanna, that there had to be something different on the routine for Kenya's Independence Day. The non-Kenyan novices too were one with us Kenyans that something had to be done. After all, wasn't Christmas Day special, when Christ was born? Or New Year's Day important, when a new year starts? This was the remembrance of a great day when Kenya was re-born, some years earlier, in 1963, or in Christian symbolism, 'born again' as a Free Nation!

As no one moved forward I decided to stick my neck out right in the middle of supper, sort of across the table and just tell Sister Joanna, (who though from Italy claimed that she was always sensitive to all things African), that the next day was an important day for us all, at least for most of us, and that we wanted some special form of commemoration. I happened to bring it up at the point during the meal when we were allowed to get into 'chat mode'. Some part of each meal time, especially lunch and supper, is spent in quiet and then also some part in listening to an extract of holy reading, before everyone is allowed to talk. Sister Joanna's antennae however picked up a totally wrong signal, something that appeared to be to her a little insubordination among the ranks. Maybe she didn't see this coming, or perhaps she thought that these holy novices had lost all sensitivity to what happened around them and that they were totally de-nationalized, or perhaps completely de-sensitized to all things human. Well, she had to think again.

On the spur of the moment she reacted rather abruptly and somewhat curtly, 'Tomorrow you will all do your study and work programme as usual. This is your novitiate programme. There is no time for celebration if you want to carry on with your novitiate training. Good night.' She then made a sign to me to stay back.

After the others had left she let loose a scathing tirade, addressing it to me of course, very much like a leader infuriated at what appeared to her to be the churlishness of her subordinates. It was Caesar, Napoleon, Alexander all rolled into one, calling the troops to order and to discipline as if a great, vital war was being lost!

When I look back today, I know that she'd really lost it! All I knew then was that I was made to feel small, humiliated and stupid. It wasn't just the content or the context of the incident. It was the public humiliation factor. She was yelling and screaming full blast perhaps more for the benefit of the 'audience' that had left the dining room than just at me. The decibels were so high that I thought some of the panes would crack. What really nearly broke was my sanity.

I feel today that her performance was not worthy of an adult trainer and definitely not proper of a senior Sister. Her accusation blasts grew louder and more vehement each time she repeated them, in language not really appropriate to a nun, so that those in the rooms around (both novices and Sisters) could hear her condemnatory proclamation. She made her point abundantly clear that she and her nuns (with their mandates and their banners fluttering high of genuine training) were delivering what was best for us 'locals' and that we ignorant ones should not even dare question the wisdom of the programmes being delivered. I said nothing as I turned cold and somewhat fearful too and felt that this was probably the end of the road for me. I know I went to bed in tears that night, and in way trembling all over somewhat fearfully and completely shaken up. I didn't get a wink of sleep. I just kept rolling in bed planning on how I could work out a 'safe' exit without alarming my parents. I had, however, to make my complaints first, in my own way.

'Why did You let that happen?' I complained to the Lord. 'I did nothing to deserve that. I was only making my point to her like any child would. Why didn't You try and make her understand? Did I do anything wrong? Am I stupid? Or has she gone off the rails? Why didn't You inspire me? I feel so afraid and friendless tonight. Will You comfort me?'

Somewhere there I seemed to feel His presence as though in a dream. 'That perhaps isn't the way to do things, Ana dear.... Just stay calm, and do your chores as you always do. Things will ease off. Trust me...I'll handle Joanna as well as can be done. You have to trust Me.'

Yet nothing that I tried to do after this, to make it up to her, worked. Sister Joanna hardened towards me. What made matters worse was that I had no one to appeal to or even discuss the matter with. Another senior Sister, Sister Francois, a French nun, who was quite a friend to me, had also gone off on sick leave, and was then transferred to another convent where it was convenient for her to get the treatment she needed. So, I was left alone. Moreover Sister Joanna was not just our Novice Mistress and our Superior. What made the situation even more horrible was the fact that she was also the Sister Consultant at the higher, Provincial Council, which had the responsibility to admit me to Vows.

I was pretty sure by now that I had met my doom. I turned gloomy and unresponsive. All my spontaneity disappeared and though Sister Joanna may have tried to deal with me professionally, it always appeared to me to be devoid of any feeling. I stopped dreaming of my future with SOS. I just curled up waiting for the end. I really thought Sister Joanna would just call me in one day, for the last time, and tell me to pack my bags. I prepared myself for that dreaded day.

I couldn't help but pray, 'Lord, guide me. I beg You. I'm helpless.' It was as if I needed to sing that inspiring hymn, 'Lead kindly light'® especially those memorable words in it, 'amid the encircling gloom....Lead Thou me on'.

In spite of the shocks I went through, the novitiate experience as a whole was indeed a time of intense prayer for me. It was a spiritual journey that seemed to be like a life I was living almost in the clouds. Perhaps it came from the constant insistence on commitment, or perhaps it was that mezzanine level I felt comfortable in, preparing me for a life of dedication. It appeared to bring up for me images of that time in the future when I would belong entirely to God. Maybe it was somewhat unrealistic as I had not really expected shocks in the middle of all the good things happening to me. It was perhaps too good to be true as an overall experience. Yet these shocks suggested that there was another narrative taking place. Maybe I was not all that aware that some tectonic plates were shifting. These encounters with Sister Joanna had sounded warning bells for me. I didn't hone in on them to develop any strategies, so when this latest tremor struck I floundered. I couldn't help but start a series of quarrels with the Lord, again!

'I just can't understand why You put me into those embarrassing situations? You know I mean well, and yet in your secret communications You seemed to say I should do things differently. Could You try and explain that a bit more? Why is Sister Joanna treating me so badly?' This was my prayerful, faith-filled request to Him, almost in total abandonment.

Of course there wasn't any audible response. Maybe it was His way of telling me He had other plans up His sleeve. Maybe this was His sort of shock treatment to wake me up from my dream-like belief that all would be well.

Sister Joanna was just looking for ways to discourage me from applying for my First Vows. The Kenya Independence day incident added to the earlier priest-crush episode and to the undue sympathy I showed to that little boy in that Nairobi encounter. These became the highlights of my Novitiate record. All this summed up became reason enough for Sister Joanna that I should think longer about my Vows. For her the decision was made. The Kenya day incident had confirmed her assessment: 'not fit for purpose', which is what she probably wrote into her notes.

She was quick to come up with her clever plan for me that I should extend my novitiate by at least another six months so as to give me a little more time to think. She would arrange for me to go to another institution where I would get involved in some work of the Order, (i.e. some more 'encounters' and other support work), and so give me time to reflect on my call to be an SOC nun. This was (her own subtle plan, I found out later) to give me time to settle down before I could perhaps continue into the Second Year of my Novitiate. She said she felt certain that I should temporarily discontinue my novitiate and definitely put off taking my Vows.

Actually for her, this was just a way of easing me out of the Order's 'systems'. It was, I thought, her final decision made. I wasn't sure though if she had discussed it with any other Senior Sister. I was in no position to question that. In my own thinking I felt there was no need for extra time. I was nearly at the end of my 2nd and final year of Novitiate, and had come through successfully in all the other procedures and training programmes. I believed I was ready for the Vows. I was quite convinced that this priest-crush and the Kenya Independence day episode were just little blips that happen to anyone, and perhaps everyone.

At times I felt emboldened to ask Sister Joanna if there hadn't been any crush in her life. I thought that if she had come through the normal or the usual way a woman grows up there must certainly have been some man in her life, or times perhaps when she did challenge some decisions made in her regard. She also had good looks and was slim and pretty, with lovely blue eyes. I noticed that European priests would come in quite often, not really on a matter of duty, for long chats with her even while she was here at her job as Novice Mistress. The lengths of these meetings seemed to take longer than those required for pure formal or just normal chats.

There were even rumours, or call them whispers, among my mates, especially the one from South Africa, that our Sister Joanna (and some of the other Sisters too) used to have quiet wine parties with one or two of the priests who visited. All this was carefully done in secluded rooms while we were at our study or at other chores. One of the Madagascar novices said she'd actually seen her hold hands, on more than one occasion, with a Spanish priest who used to give us talks. One of the Kenyan novices said Joanna had probably been more involved. Once soon after our Spanish priest had been there, this novice had been sent to clean up one of the rooms in the Sisters' area, which had wine glasses and a beer bottle lying around, and also some cigarette stubs which the Sisters probably forgotten to remove. Yet I really didn't want to dwell on all that, nor did I want to bring up occasions when she raised her voice in issuing orders to the Junior Sister in charge of us when things didn't go that smoothly in their relationships.

Whatever might have been the case, I was determined that I would apply for my vows and that I was not going to take the extra time. I couldn't help but enter my quarrel-zone again.

'What's all this happening to me?' I pleaded. 'You know that I want to serve You. I don't need this extra time. I feel I'm ready. I've done enough. Can't You convince her that I'm ready? You know I'm ready. You know that the crush I had on that priest has all gone. It was just a temporary blip. I can't see it coming back. Also, you know that I'm not really challenging Sister when I disagree with things. It's just my stubbornness perhaps, or perhaps the sense of always challenging injustice deep inside me. You are my Lord, my only Bridegroom. I love You. I trust You as I've always done. I want You to guide me and take care of me...Do something about this, please!'

In spite of the confidence shown in my quarrels, I felt that He and I were at cross purposes. I don't know what it was but I was not getting it. I kept praying but there seemed to be only emptiness in my thoughts. It was only irritating me more. There were days when all my prayer seemed meaningless and routine. I thought the Lord was losing interest in my plans. I just felt I had to have recourse to my appeals much oftener so as to be able to see some light at the end of the tunnel.

'Can't You at least give me some sign that I feel I can always do the right thing? Why have You left me floundering like this? Please don't play games with me. I can't take it anymore. I'm losing interest in everything. I can't help telling you I'm a bit annoyed with You right now. Yes, show me some sign. I need your help badly. Show up please!' I pleaded.

I kept praying a lot but didn't receive any audible reply of course. And then suddenly, almost out of the blue, my friend and adviser, Father Lucien, from Mavoko, the one who had helped me to join up the SOC, quite unexpectedly decided to drop by just to see how I was doing. I couldn't believe my luck. I knew the Lord had something to do with my friend's turning up.

Chapter 7: A time to speak: Making decisions

I was almost on the point of giving in to the constant pressures and probing efforts of Sister Joanna seemingly trying to help me by suggesting I should delay my First Vows. I was in this confused state of mind when Father Lucien came by. Besides looking after his assignments and his pastoral work in parishes and institutions of his Order he also cared for poor young boys especially, getting them on to training courses. I liked to call his Order the Priests of the Slums® (POS) rather than their longish name connected with some bearded Saint from the south of Europe, something Father Lucien always seems to get annoyed about. Some of these priests might have got lead roles in Danny Boyle's® Slumdog Millionaire®. They actually do good, constructive vocational training for youth, some of them picked up from the streets or others who are dropouts from schools.

The POS, like the other great Orders --the Comboni, the Consolata, the White Fathers-- do selfless work for the underprivileged and the needy, especially young people. Father Lucien had been a good friend and advisor to me while we were at Mavoko and had given me invaluable help in guiding me all along during my difficult days. He has been one of those friends in life who has been a blessing, probably sent to me as the 'advising angel', maybe as a sort of response to some of the quarrels I've always had with the Lord.

'So, what do you think, Father Lucien?' I asked him. 'Should I delay my Vows?'

'I don't think you should. I think this nun has already made up her mind. She is only putting you off, almost to cover her back for the not-so-kind way in which she has treated you. From what you tell me I think she has not discussed this with others in her convent, or probably not even with her Superiors at the higher level. I think you should just go ahead with what your conscience tells you to do,' said Father.

'You really think that she's playing games with me?'

'Yes, to a point I think that's what she is doing. All that has happened to you, as you've been telling me, even in your letters, only indicates quite a normal progression of one in the Novitiate. You're going through a period of uncertainty, which is what is supposed to happen in the novitiate. This is absolutely normal for novices.'

'You really think so, Father?'

'Yes. I think that you should apply for your Vows. Just go ahead. Let your application go through the usual process. There will be wiser people in the Provincial Council. I feel the team of Council Members cannot reject your application. Even if she is against you there will be a majority vote, and I feel you'll come through.'

'You really believe this, Father?'

'Yes, I do. Now what do *you* really feel about it? Do you feel *you* are ready?' he asked.

'Yes, Father. I feel I am ready in every way, determined to become a member of the SOC. I feel I have gone through the entire training sincerely and have equipped myself for my Vows and for my future work. I feel I'm ready to apply for the Vows.'

That proved to be a sort of massive vote of support for me. I trusted Father Lucien's judgement immensely. He had guided me along for so many years and had dealt with problems of other young people too who had joined up Orders of nuns and priests, and had offered them wise solutions. I always felt comfortable talking to him. I felt he was probably right this time too.

Not that I distrusted his opinion in any way, but I felt I had to take some other soundings too. My novice mate, Sheila, from South Africa was a few years older to me. She had also gone through a rare experience of having left an Order at the beginning of a Novitiate. She had been for about two years with the Daughters of Mary Order® (DOM) in Zimbabwe. They were an Order that looked after girls and mothers with unwanted pregnancies. She didn't feel comfortable with that programme, and being of a literary mind and a good speaker trained in religious discussions, she felt the SOC calling was hers. She had gone through her postulant training in South Africa and in Zimbabwe and was now completing the Novitiate with me in Kenya.

We were good friends, and I was really close to her. When I discussed my uncertainties and revealed my sort of crush earlier on a priest, she comforted me and also confided in me by telling me she too had had a relationship, a little more than what I had experienced. She had gone through at least one boyfriend in school, and later even as a postulant in Zimbabwe she had had a crush on a Religious Brother. They had been placed together almost accidentally, she told me, to attend to a pregnant girl who was a refugee who had needed help. The Brother who was slightly her senior was assigned to help out in a sort of Mentor-Support role.

Their work brought them together quite a few times. On the third occasion that they had met she was able to give him some strong hints that she had been charmed by his kindness and by the intelligent way in which he handled situations. She even said that she felt she wanted to work with him on other projects. She told him that he had put some sort of a spark in their working relationship. Short of telling him that she really liked him, and loved him perhaps, she must certainly have made him feel that he was more than just a friend or a colleague.

On a fourth occasion when they met she found herself getting really close to him, even physically. She wanted to touch his hand, and made efforts to sit right beside him on the sofa in the sitting room, in the Centre, where they professionally discussed the problems regarding the case they were handling. He may have noticed this, or perhaps he was pleased that she was indeed relishing his company and his lead role. She felt drawn to him, as she sat close to him that particular evening. At one point, she literally stopped talking to him or taking notice of what they were discussing professionally. During that feedback session she just kept staring at him, seemingly listening keenly, to all he had to say, but with almost no response, with her eyes drooping, almost drooling over him.

Usually she went off earlier or later than him after their project work, but on this fifth occasion she couldn't resist asking him to accompany him on the bus for the 90-minute bus journey back to her place. She just wanted the closeness of his company for that one-hour ride before he got off at his centre. It was like gold dust for him. He had asked her on earlier occasions to get on the bus with him but she had always thought it prudent not to travel with him, eager to separate business from friendship. However, on that day she felt different. She felt all charged up emotionally, with her feminine side taking control of her feelings. She was sure that nothing would stop her from being near him. She just had to be with him on that bus. The sensual side of her was brimming over, and she believed that he was her 'man'. Her feelings were running ahead of her.

It was late evening when the two of them sat next to each other in the back rows of the dimly-lit bus. He too felt he had begun to like her presence and to appreciate all her suggestions in their professional work. In the light of the fading sun sneaking into the bus he noticed her nudging closer to him as he sat near the last window of that country-lane bus. Soon both of them became aware that as they kept squeezing each other's hands they were actually releasing powerful unspoken messages that had been stored in zip files.

The silence helped these vibes to get transmitted into a form that both seemed to understand and to relish. There was no mistaking the fact that they had both decoded their longings. Their hearts for certain now beat faster, and in unison. It wasn't long before his arms were around her, and at an opportune moment she couldn't resist her first real kiss. Unnoticed by the other passengers, on that dusky evening, they were also able to show more intimacy. She had never experienced these feelings before and couldn't believe that his hands made her feel that she was really loved and cared for. She had longed for protection and for care, and had always kept her feelings bottled. Yet now, almost unseen and unnoticed in the corner of that bus, she felt safe to let her feelings be known, to say that she wanted love and protection. She wanted him. She switched off as she snuggled up closer to him.

Of course once they reached destination, the 'passionate holds' had to switch back to 'cool off' mode, at least physically. She soon realized that she had got carried away and that it had been one of her unusual hormonal spills. Reflecting on it later she felt convinced that it was all a little emotional storm in a teacup. She then told me that, as compared to her 'bus fare' and her wild uncontrollable response, my crush on that priest was not even skin-deep. She insisted that I go ahead and apply for my Vows, because I looked much more committed now than she had been at that point in her life.

I wanted to know more so I kept prodding her. 'You mean you've forgotten all that? And you even kissed? You mean it all cooled off?'

'Yes, we're human. These things happen. I didn't forget about it all immediately. It took a little time, but I did some serious reflection in my quieter and more sensible moments and, when I had calmed down, I knew I had to forget it all...I also did some special chats, a retreat® actually, with a senior priest to make sure I was on the right path. It did me a lot of good to help me straighten up.'

'What about that Brother? How did he take it?' I had to ask.

'Oh, he? Well, he was an experienced guy. He told me later, when the sensual excitement in the bus had cooled down, that he had had a crush on others too. He didn't want to give me details, but it would seem that he had wanted to go further with me. He revealed that in the course of our meetings he had developed a fondness for me and suggested meeting up another time somewhere. He even mentioned a hotel scene, sort of half-way between our two places of residence, a kind of outdoor tavern, where we could meet up occasionally, or regularly perhaps, to see how we could get closer. He also revealed that he had pursued a postulant of another Order, with whom he said he had gone a longer distance, whatever that meant. They had gone through two dates and had kissed a few times, and had got quite passionate too. Later he heard that she had left the convent in the hope of linking up with him. Somehow he got cold feet and would not leave his Order. So she was left high and dry. He stayed on in his training, and she was left abandoned. He was honest enough to admit this to me.'

'Was he fully trained? Did he have vows?' I was eager to find out.

'Oh yes. He had been a Brother already with Temporary® Vows, for two years. He was supposed to have been mentoring me. In a cynical way I could see his gentler side when his hands felt me all over so soothingly and caringly when we were in the bus. It was an incredibly pleasurable feeling I can't easily forget as a woman. Yes, he did exploit my softer side. Somehow I hadn't realized that side of me and I just lost control of myself temporarily. I didn't realize during those moments that the woman inside me would always be there. Yet I feel so ashamed of the incident now.'

'Where's he now?' I was curious to know.

'Well, as you might imagine, he had enough courage to find a good counsellor who advised him to leave, as religious life was not the place for him. The Vows were not for him.'

'So, did he meet up with the nun who left the convent for him?' I asked.

'I don't know....It's possible he did, but I didn't follow up his case.'

'Have you met up with him since?'

'No. He's in Zimbabwe, and I'm here. Also, I don't think I'll meet him unless of course he comes my way, or I happen to land up in Zimbabwe.'

'Do you get any sort of wild memories of him now and then? Does it throw you off a bit, perhaps during your prayers or meditations?'

'Not really. I soon sussed out that he knew I was young and vulnerable, with my womanhood just blossoming. He admitted that he was quite hot-blooded with his testosterone levels peaking. He also revealed that if I had got off with him on that bus ride, he would not have hesitated to have gone the distance with me, down in some bushes, as he found me ravishing and almost longing for physical satisfaction. At that point we were just two consenting adults ready for a sensual adventure. He found me letting myself go and freely responding to his soothing advances. I might have been in real trouble then, and may perhaps have changed course. He confessed though that he was just playing with me, getting his own sort of kick out of it all. I'm glad I got out of his clutches, and so glad I didn't become his victim.'

'What really helped you come out of it?' I had to ask.

'My better judgement, and someone praying for me (perhaps my mother), must have got me back to my senses. It would have been a real disaster for me, if I had even dreamt of getting off that bus with him. Even that other postulant he had in his sights was only

81

someone he wanted to have some fun with. He wasn't serious about her though he seems to have had some sort of an affair with her, when she had gone on vacation, in her house, very much like when you met that priest on a holiday. Coming to think of it now, he really wasn't worth a second thought, and I knew it was just a little blip in my commitment to God. I think I forgot for a moment that I was vulnerable as a woman. Occasionally I do get very angry with myself for being so naive. I should have known better.'

'Do you have regrets?'

'No, none at all. As I said, I knew it was just a moment of weakness. God forgives and then strengthens us. You shouldn't be afraid. You'll be fine.'

I couldn't have asked for more helpful advice. I was just determined now to apply for my Vows. I went back to the same resolve after Father Lucien had spoken to me.

Chapter 8: A time to plant: Moving on

Though that encounter with Sister Joanna had left a bitter taste in my mouth I still felt the Lord was on my side. I tried to live as normal a life as I had been doing all through my Novitiate years. Yet somehow I felt that there was something not quite right. I couldn't put my finger on it but I felt that the Lord was possibly trying to play games with me. So I plucked up enough courage to tackle Him one day, in my usual style.

'I hope You're looking after me properly. I think there's something you're hiding from me. Tell me. Don't give me some rude shock. I don't feel strong enough to take on any more than I've had. I know You care for me but of late You're not entirely showing me your hand. You always seem to have the trump card. But try and understand my situation. Let's play a fair game. I need your help really, to stay calm, to stay sane.' I thought I'd said it all.

I kept praying like this for many days in a row. During this time I found Sister Joanna getting farther and farther away from me. I could sense something was brewing, and yet I kept trying to be my usual self: cheery and bubbly with all my mates, getting on with my chores.

Yet somehow I had this feeling that something would happen. One day towards the end of my second year of Novitiate, while I was doing my usual laundry chores, I was sent for by Sister Joanna. I sensed that this was probably it. It was. I felt cold and tense even before I got to her office.

'I have an important message for you from the Council: You should not take your Vows,' she said in a cool, emotionless, calculated statement. I was stunned and speechless.

'But......but... what about my... my application?' I dared to ask in quite a tremulous voice.

'The Council has rejected your application.' She spoke with continued control and sternness.

'So....so.... what... what happens now?' I sort of managed to speak with my eyes moist, and with my heart wanting to explode. I was wild with anger and frustration. 'What...what... do I do now?'

'I suppose you'll have to go home,' was her cold instruction, with her eyes looking in the distance, almost afraid to face me. 'Get your things ready soon, and make arrangements to leave.'

Though I was expecting a verdict something like that I couldn't take it when it came. It was like a landslide that takes away everything in its path. It was as if my entire digestive system had been flushed out. I was in total shock. I didn't know what to think, what to say or what to do. That was at the end of May 1996, a week before the feast of Pentecost®. I had no choice. Sister Joanna spoke with all the powers invested in her, not just like Pilate® washing her hands off me, but like Herodias® wanting my head on a plate! Crest-fallen, dejected and frustrated, I left the Novitiate the next day. With my dream now in tatters I was like a castaway, with no plans, no hope and possibly no future.

I was shattered and totally broken. I went home and just refused to speak to anyone. It was such an odd situation for me. Even my younger sister, Adreya, was working but I had no such hope of a position in life, after all those 'postulant years', apparently fruitless in worldly terms. The nuns had left me on the rocks. They not only did not give me any recommendation or any 'petty cash' to live, but they also told outlets of the Order, like their centres in Kenya and in Tanzania (I found out later), that they should not entertain me. It was as if I had become a criminal, or perhaps an outcast. The other novices I was leaving behind were also warned that they were not to communicate with me for the foreseeable future. I couldn't imagine that nuns could become so cruel and so heartless. My nun fantasy had definitely collapsed! What was my crime? Was she the 'Idi Amin'® of the convent? What had I done to merit this terrible treatment? I could only take refuge in the fact that Christ too had suffered rejection and even crucifixion for no fault of His. I tried to get back to my complaints, but just didn't have the unction to do so right then.

In spite of being rock bottom in confidence and frustrated to say the least, I finally plucked up enough courage some days later when back home to re-start my dialogues with the Lord. I don't know how I did it. The Order, in some ways an institution of the Church, had literally abandoned me, and I felt the Lord had not been totally honest with me. Or was I deluded?

'Where have You been? I'm all alone. No money, no friends, no one to support me. You've abandoned me. I thought it was all going so well until suddenly this massive meteorite crashed into my planet. This is all a rude shock, and I can't see your guiding hand anywhere. There's no lighthouse in all this darkness on really high seas. I'm lost, totally confused and am much like a rudderless ship. Can't You see that I need You just now?' In the middle of all that I just couldn't see any voice talking to me, or any inspiration cheering me on.

Yet to my utter surprise at home everyone was sweet and kind to me. My family embraced me back with open arms and with no preconditions. Yet I spent several nights just crying away hoping to blank out all that intensity of frustration, desperation and despair. However, in reality I didn't cry all that much. It was more choking and anger with spurts of profuse crying. Women in our cultures in fact don't cry as much as those in others. We internalise a lot. Even at funerals people don't scream or cry loudly. We try and link our frustrations into what we are doing. That's exactly what I was striving to do. Mum and Dad though were truly the angels that God put in place for me. My dad was truly 'apostolic', if I can use the word here, and comforted me more than any priest or counsellor might have done.

'The nuns didn't really send you away, my dear,' he told me. 'They sent you home. This is your home. Feel at home. We're here for you. We love you. It will all be well. Just relax, my girl.'

I could not believe that Mum too was so loving and tender, and kept saying, 'You're still my girl, my darling. I'm here for you. We'll find something for you to do. Life is still yours. All is not lost. Stay calm and relax at home. You're my girl.'

Yet it was all too much for me. More than anything else I felt humiliated. When I'd gone to join the convent I had left everything behind: my closest friends, my society contacts, my professional development. I had fallen in love with Christ, and I never expected that He would let me in for this rude awakening, with all my supports gone, my dreams shattered! Every one of my mates had moved on ahead. They were all at least 5 years ahead of me in work, in society, in progress. I felt left out, left behind. 'Where do I begin?' sang Maria in the Sound of Music®. Maria had the Von Trapp family to try her luck again. I only felt trapped by the abandonment of the SOC and the Voice of the Lord that I could not clearly hear in that confused transmission of sound waves. Maria had a slither of hope of being in the company of the Baron Von Trapp she had grown to love. I had nothing. I hadn't cultivated boyfriends in my youth, and now even that priest-crush was a little more than an orange-squash I had hurriedly gulped down. I had gone off with a bang, I had returned with a thud.

How could I start again? I had no skills except learning to do chores like laundry, cleaning, singing psalms, praying at different times. I had no skills that the world needed. I knew I had to start all over again if I wanted to make something of myself. It was like a little girl trying to climb Mount Kenya® without proper shoes or supporting equipment, or any training. It is true I was still young and perhaps somewhat attractive, but there's a stigma to girls who leave a convent. Would men give me a second look? Girls who leave the convent are FGs (Failed Girls), or perhaps somewhat unsteady characters. Of course that could be a plus-point for hot-blooded males. We (at least most of us I believe) are still virgins when we leave the convent. That is a massive plus in African society, and definitely in the Akamba list of values! That part of the woman in me began trying to stick its head out of the snail-shell. Or should I have tried another Order as one of my mates had done?

There was more on my plate than I could handle. Would employers give me even an apprentice position to start life anew? How far would laundry work, singing and praying skills take me? It was also a spiritual crisis. I felt dry in prayer and just didn't want to think of going to church or meeting up with even my close neighbours. I just buried myself at home very much like the ostrich! It was in space flight terms, 'no systems go'.

Chapter 9: A time to mourn: The Family in turmoil

Soon after I left the convent there was another tragedy that hit me deeply. We were a close-knit family and my brothers and sisters were close to me. They had grown up well, under the careful and loving care of Mum and Dad. It is not always easy though to keep track of grown-up children, especially when they move from their teens to being adults. One of my brothers, Antyn, and one of my sisters, Anesa, got unduly influenced by a senior relative in the family.

Sometimes within the family there are subtle connections that cannot be understood or fathomed, or perhaps controlled. I still cannot understand how in such a devout family as ours, all church-going, deeply Catholic and committed, there could have been a member, Mum's younger brother, (i.e. my uncle Jonas), who developed patterns of behaviour that defy explanation. He was an uncle dear to all of us. He shared our table, our joys and our togetherness, but so did Judas at the Last Supper table. Judas had as his mates perhaps members the most elite club in the world, the Apostles®, chosen by Christ to live with Him and share His life. But he defaulted. He betrayed Christ to the Jewish leaders who wanted Him for falsified charges of transgressing their laws.

Somewhere down the line, not very different from Judas in the Bible, Jonas veered off the narrow but straight path to heaven. Or perhaps, at some point in time, he had shrewdly begun to play a double game: one for his family and one for his interests. If a double personality could have existed in Christ's inner circle, I guess it could have happened anywhere. Where the influences came from I am still not able to find out but Jonas got involved in some sort of a cult, not sure if it was 'theistic' or 'atheistic'. Or was it perhaps just the 'voices' within him that formed themselves into a belief that urged him on to devious ways? I did hear Antyn, my brother, speak of some 'voices' giving him instructions when we lived together for a time, but I paid no attention to this thinking it was all something delusional and just a passing fantasy. At that point I never imagined that it was even a crisis in his beliefs as he was quite strong mentally, someone you couldn't easily convince to do something you wanted. Moreover he was generally alright with his work and his life.

The European 'enlightenment' brought in, even in works such as Milton's 'Paradise Lost' and the works of the English Romantic poets, a certain crisis of faith that broadened out into theories of individualism and free will in wider society. These trends made the Biblical temptations of Christ and the 'possession' stories look like allegories. This licence led to a set of beliefs which developed into a cult in Ohio, USA, in 1948. In 1969 an 'atheistic' Church was founded by LaVey®. Soon 'theistic' churches followed. There was a hint of atheism trends even in the writings of Bernard Shaw and Mark Twain.

From western trends in fashion, admin systems (and of course later the internet), these trends just flowed from the 'western' world, especially the USA, through into Africa, Asia, Latin America and elsewhere. Young people especially those wanting to express themselves freely as human beings, even in Kenya, found these atheistic trends and cults a convenient bandwagon. In a world of conformism to laws, to society, to Church, misguided and ill-informed folk found these beliefs (or whatever they understood of them) a haven for individuality and creativity. What these 'believers' were not able to fathom, whether they were drug-addicts or not, was that there were pitfalls and slippery slopes that could take effect, very much like those resulting from the small print on documents and policies that are not carefully read. A friend of mine, for example, when visiting in Mumbai, was lured away for three days, by one of these cult groups. The powerful 'Midday' paper there helped to get her released from the clutches of this group. Details of the incident seemed to show that this group functioned very much in the way these cults seemed to be operating in Kenya. However I still cannot imagine how these beliefs could have seeped through into my family.

It is interesting to note also that Kenya is ranked 15th in Africa in its people's belief in witchcraft , a few points behind the Congo, but way ahead of Ethiopia, Nigeria, Zambia and Rwanda. A quarter of Kenyans, Christians and others, confessed they believe in the protective power of juju (charms or amulets) and that they consult traditional healers. Atheism strangely enough does not really dabble in witchcraft and charms even if there is no fine dividing line. I never, for instance, noticed members of my family, friends or neighbours, even believing in elements of witchcraft, let alone atheism. However almost without my being aware of it some realities were going to change for me too.

In Kenya these atheistic groups are not easily identified and in one of these twists of life my uncle Jonas became a 'follower' of what was perhaps a cult. I was never able to find out how and why he got involved nor what his activities were. All I eventually came to know was that he influenced two of my younger siblings, Antyn and Anesa.

Antyn grew up as a happy, intelligent boy. He was top of his class all through his 8 years at Primary school. My parents sent him to boarding school, actually a seminary high school, in Embu®, in the north of Kenya. He excelled there both in his behaviour as well as in his studies and activities, passing out in flying colours in Form 4 (Grade 10 equivalent) exams. My years away from home did not really let me into his secrets as we were both apart, he in high school and I in the SOC. As I was recovering from my post-SOC trauma I managed to convince Dad to send him to Accountancy school, when he had just turned 18, soon after he was back from seminary school. He then stayed with me, when I'd returned from the convent, as his college was just a walking distance away. I now got to know him a bit better and we tried to catch up on the years we had been apart. We were fond of each other and though we got on well, as I look back now, I don't think I really got into his thoughts. All I can remember of him was that he was dependable and responsible. He would cook, clean up and go shopping, and generally look after our little place in Nairobi.

However, after a while I noticed a sudden change in Antyn, soon after he got into work. We were not able to meet up that often. From being very religious he became anti-religious. He stopped attending church, and when questioned by me he said he felt 'de-christianized' by the forced worship routines in seminary school. Perhaps he was trying to express a deeper reaction than just one to religious practices. He soon changed again after about a year that he had got into work, and then became a religious 'adict', if I can use the term. He would even sit and discuss the sermon at the Mass we went to together. We couldn't afford individual DVD/CD players, earlier when we were together, and so we listened to music together. I liked gospel music, some reggae and of course Madonna, while Antyn's tastes were rock or radical reggae. I also found out that his choice of movies was pretty narrow. I found he liked movies with horror or violence which he often described to me in great detail. He just couldn't miss an episode of X Files, for instance.

A month before he met his tragic end, in November, he had come to visit me in Mavoko. I noticed that there was a sombre expression on his face, but there wasn't the least clue that he was sanely and methodically preparing to end his life. I did my best to get him to talk but he was always so playful with me that I couldn't get through to him. It felt as though he was being controlled by some external forces. Were these the 'voices' that a lot of people seem to hear? Or were there some messages he was getting from the 'hidden circles' my uncle had introduced him to? I'll never know.

I only found out he didn't meet up with his friends as he used to, and would spend hours in loneliness or just in listening to crazy music. Soon after he had passed away I went to the little flat we had shared in Nairobi to try and get some clues. I found nothing. He had probably carefully destroyed anything that could have served as evidence. There must have been a line of communication between him and someone else who may have warned him about this too, it would seem.

We never found out. He was certainly getting himself ready for what he had in plan, his fatal dramatic finale.

It looks like we may never find out why Antyn took his life on that January morning. He was healthy, humorous, intelligent and successful. He had come to spend a few days with us. One of those days, in Mavoko, when we were all going to Church for Sunday Mass he set out with us, and then quite unexpectedly turned back saying he had forgotten something at home. We went on walking to Church, which wasn't a long way from home. After a while when we didn't see him following us, my mum went back to check what was delaying him. That of course took her a good quarter of an hour.

She couldn't find him in the house, which was locked. She kept searching and then to her horror, when checking the hut where we kept our animals, she found him lying unconscious on the floor. He was still holding the bottle which we found later to contain a powerful concoction of insecticides and pesticides mixed with coke. By the time she had alerted the neighbours his life was gone. There was probably only about 30 minutes between him leaving the group and my mum finding him, but it was just 30 minutes too late for any recovery from that lethal dose he chose to drink.

He also had a sweet girlfriend. What is surprising is that he didn't leave any suicide note. He only left a letter for his girlfriend which we were able to find before it could be delivered to her. He wrote, 'Don't mourn for me. You need to complete your studies. Please let go of me, and find love in another man's arms....If there is love where I am going, I will love you forever.'

In the house I discovered a few capsules containing a white substance. These were so big that they could not be swallowed. We sent those to a government chemist for testing but they weren't any of the abused substances we know of. That ruled out drugs. I thought HIV and AIDS could have depressed him but none of his close friends could back that theory. Moreover he was medically healthy. I guess the causes of his death will remain a mystery.

My sister, Anesa, younger to Antyn had an even worse episode. Towards the end of a harrowing time trying to get her to see sense, because she had become unbelievably unruly, when she was only 15, she revealed to us that our uncle Jonas had got both her and Antyn inducted into a cult, which we surmised later had something to do with atheism. She couldn't really explain its beliefs but felt it was giving her independence and confidence. She was always a rebellious child and putting her into boarding school after Antyn's death, when she was around 13, didn't really help.

She said that uncle had got her into these beliefs ever since she was in Standard 6, or at just about 10 years of age. She said she had grown addicted to it and needed to see uncle on a regular basis to feel guided and encouraged. Uncle lived with our grandmother, some distance away from us all, and that put an additional strain on our resources and on our time. In a way it seemed to split our family into two camps.

It was only through Mum's constant prayers and gentle persuasion that we were able to take Anesa for counselling and cleansing. She kept reporting that 'voices' spoke to her ordering her to do things in a particular way. Once during her time of holiday from school Mum had convinced her to go to a charismatic® retreat®. That probably was a turning point for her. It took close to 3 years after that, with professional help, before Anesa was fully healed. She is fine now, pursuing a successful career.

My uncle's behaviour and style of life still remain the enigma as, besides drifting into forms of atheism with such a strong Catholic background and upbringing, he also masterminded an entire plot almost to de-Christianise the family. He revealed quite ominously in the middle of all the mourning that went on after Antyn's shocking death where he too shed copious tears that this death was only the beginning of other things to happen. We must thank God that he didn't live to see other demonizing events he may have had in the making. The family gradually recovered its former Christian equilibrium and we got closer together as a family, even though it will take us a lifetime to come to terms with my brother's passing away. Strangely enough we do not talk about or seem to miss our uncle, who passed away two years after Antyn. We are also truly delighted that we were able to bring Anesa back into the fold.

Chapter 10: A time to weep: Going off at a tangent

It took a long time for me to accept the loss of Antyn. I tried a lot of therapies and strategies but nothing really seemed to be working for me. I remained disconsolate and disoriented. I just couldn't find any explanations. In the middle of that confused state one person came by who helped to lift me, at least partly, out of this depressing gloom. The one who dropped by constantly and who in many ways was there for me was a seminarian in the last year of his theology® studies. He showed what I thought was true empathy. He was different. He was kind and treated me gently.

We spent several hours together talking and generally conversing on a variety of topics. I liked his views and what is more I began to like him as a person and as someone who seemed to be truly human. I soon found myself holding his hands even when walking around. That familiarity grew and things developed so quickly that before I could try to assess the situation he had become a frequent visitor to our house. He too began to fancy me quite a bit and even as I was trying to come to grips with the loss of my brother he seemed to be there for me. He found time to be with me as often as he could. It so happened that the placement for his training was not far from where we lived and so it became easy for us to meet up. I thought that was a blessing in disguise.

When trying to get a grip on things I seemed to lose control of what was happening. I can't really explain how it all happened. However, Ashley, this seminarian, had it all worked out. I got so immersed in this release and relief that came by so gratuitously that I somehow did not try very hard to find out more about him. His presence was so relaxing and encouraging. It was a kind of a similar situation, though a more intense version, of the time I'd fallen for that priest who had visited us at home. Yet there was a sort of a difference. I believed in the fact that if he was in his last year of theology, which is just a year before taking Holy Orders, he must certainly have ticked all the boxes for his trainers and must have been a good person. Moreover, as he was not yet a priest it sort of seemed permissible that I could at least attempt to be openly friendly with him. Yet I was not perfectly sure I could go further and date him.

However, now that I was in more ways than one a free bird (not a postulant any more), I thought I could test the waters and see if indeed I could at least share some of my deeper, inner thoughts. Mum, always shrewd in her judgements and always protective, sounded quiet warnings. She noticed I was getting close to Ashley and seemed to have some reservations. Senior women always have this sixth sense. Mum didn't particularly like him. I too made little effort to try and probe questions to him that might have told me something more about him, about his status or about what his intentions might have been.

He was from Tanzania and was completing his theology studies in a Nairobi institution. He was based in a little place of his Order, in the Mavoko area, not far from where we lived. All I really knew about him was that he would, in time, return to Tanzania to his ministry. I never once asked him what his plans were or why he was taking so much interest in me and in my family. His language was always coated in a lot of church jargon, rich in Biblical and theological vocabulary. I felt blown over by it all. He also certainly knew how to be gentle with a woman. That perhaps was the final straw that made me trust him. He really knew how to get to my softer side. Moreover I wasn't aware that he had known me for quite some time. Apparently he had actually spotted me in the convent during my novitiate days and had kept an eye on me ever since. I didn't know that he had taken a real fancy to me then. It was actually more than just a crush, he revealed later.

So, would I trust him? I fell head over heels in love with him. Emotions clouded my imagination and clear thinking. He however had it all worked out, almost to the last detail. I was really naive, and hadn't really understood what sensual feelings can do to one's sanity and reason. He on the other hand had studied me in detail, all my feelings, my needs and my weaknesses. My only experience of dealing with someone I liked or loved was that one occasion I had had with that priest during a holiday when I'd come for a visit during my novitiate. It was too brief and too disconnected from the life I was leading. I hadn't really stopped to analyse it carefully. He was a good guy, a priest aware of his position. Ashley though was a different proposition. He had it all calculated almost to the last detail. He had timed it all to one evening when my parents and all my brothers and sisters were away at some gathering. He came in suavely dressed and heavily perfumed, seductively touching and holding me, and then gently luring me into his arms. I just fell into his embrace.

That evening we were two consenting adults enjoying uncontrolled passion. I felt I had released during all those long and powerful intense minutes all my womanly feelings that had lain there unexplored. It was my first real experience, and a costly one too as I'd let my virginity go almost without a bargain! Though it was spontaneous, exciting, memorable and exhausting, the painful thrill soon had to simmer down to serious thoughts. Even though the passion seemed to linger on for quite a long while after, I was really in a confused state of flux, trying to get back to my logical thinking and planning!

I was new to it all as a woman but I knew that somewhere along that encounter I had taken on a new responsibility, and had possibly crossed another rite of passage! The advice I got, from friends who stood by me, had me believing that I ought to take relief in the great Akamba traditions, because indeed I had crossed another threshold: a possible pregnancy that meant motherhood. I had suddenly moved to a new stage of my life. Whatever the implications, the involvement and the excitement, I knew I had to face the fact that I was alone again, uncertain of the future.

I later came to know that Ashley was quite experienced at all this. He seemed to come out of it quite satisfied and relieved that he had won his prize. What I didn't notice then was that he played down his dominant role. He made me feel good about my releasing the woman in me, something he had been working on in subtle ways and moves over quite a long time. Yet there weren't two ways about it. He had achieved his objective: not sure whether it was pleasure or progeny. I wasn't very sure I knew what I had achieved.

All I knew was that I would be pregnant, which again blissfully is a blessing for any African woman. I had in a way sealed my position in the tribe. This part of it certainly felt good even though I was quite firm at one time earlier in my life of not giving away my virginity. The memory of all those great saints like Maria Goretti defending her virginity did flash up a sort of danger signal, but my Akamba pride seemed to come to my rescue to swallow all that and find rational explanations. In any case at this point I had to face new realities.

When the pregnancy became apparent I had of course to tell my mother and the family. It was a difficult decision: keep the baby, or abort. I decided to keep the baby and Mum supported me all the way. I couldn't help but turn to Akamba ways where any pregnancy is to be treasured as a blessing from God. Here my Christian failure of a clandestine affair suddenly took second place over the Akamba joy of a new life being brought into the world. I had to convince myself that this was more than just the only rational way forward. It was as if I had been awoken from sleep to find life had changed for me, forever. It was as if the Lord came by to say, 'Hey, Anna...here's something to think about, seriously.'

Soon after that, however, I noticed that Ashley's visits subsequent to the affair were fewer. He still maintained his closeness to me and his promises that he would do the world for me. He said that he would go ahead temporarily with his theology studies but would then at the appropriate time leave to be with me, so that both of us could be together. We discussed briefly that we would then tie the knot and regularise our marriage. As events moved on he had to return to Tanzania for the last part of his ministerial experience. He would then, as he had promised, leave all that and return to me. I naively believed all that but the reality proved to be different.

I nearly went into overdrive, and complained to the Lord. 'Where has he gone? Can't You convince him to at least come by to help me out? I feel so lost, so unsupported. Can't You see that? Can't You help me, please?'

I really missed Ashley's support those final days of pregnancy, the 4 months before I was due. I tried to keep in touch with him by phone but the calls were short and he never spoke a lot. He didn't keep calling me as I had expected, or indeed as he had promised.

To make matters worse, I had, as a Catholic, to go to confession, to confess to the affair. The priest in the confessional asked me some probing questions which quite annoyed me. I didn't think he was gentle or fatherly enough to try and understand me. When I stopped giving answers he began turning the screw on me, quite in an 'ecclesiastical' and threatening way, saying he could not give me absolution if certain conditions were not met. I didn't know how I could resolve the difficult situation and he didn't really offer advice. I felt abandoned. I think I've never been so angry in my life. In a moment of frustration I left the confessional. I guess the priest was bewildered but at that moment I really didn't care about what he thought.

Back home I went into complaint mode: 'Why did You let that happen, Lord? I thought that priest was terrible. Did You put all those words into his mouth? I don't believe he could tell me so many things and give me such an overdose of warnings. You mean You don't forgive? Or did I hear it all wrong? I wish You could communicate with me in person, or, give me someone I can talk to.' That at least helped release some tension from my system.

As events unfolded I became wiser. I found out that Ashley had proceeded with his plans and didn't want to have anything to do with me. It was clear now that he had only wanted to have fun with me. I didn't know if he was now using his ministerial privileges and his Biblical jargon to undo other women. That was something the Lord would have to handle. Right now I had to deal with my pregnancy. That was a new chapter in my life. It would seem that the Lord knew how to test me and yet keep control of me. I kept praying that I would get a baby girl, as it is commonly believed that they give fewer problems medically. A girl it was, but born prematurely. She was for months in an incubator, and her life was literally hanging in the balance. I didn't want to lose her. I hit the panic button. I just had to complain to Him to save my child.

'Now what's all this? You gave me a hard time at confession. Then Ashley walked out of my life. I thought that at least You would support my baby. No. You had to have me deliver earlier. It's true You gave me a girl, but will she survive? I'm keeping my fingers crossed You will do the right thing for me. Will You? I'm going to call her Faith.' That sort of settled my nerves a bit.

I spent many nights in tears while I watched beside my child, Faith, who was first in the incubator and then in intensive care. I've become over-protective. Just can't help it. It's a whole new experience: being a mother. This time He seemed to listen to me. Faith came out alright, finally, and is growing up nicely. She's my pride and joy now, eight years on. I'm hoping

He'll give me time to see her through college and university. He can take me then.

Chapter 11: A time to gather: Picking up the pieces

When I was sent back from the novitiate I was in the eyes of society a reject case. Ex-nuns, or ex-postulants, are not looked upon favourably. I actually saw the situation of (Sister) Sabine. Now I was in it myself. I held my head in shame. I was a failure. I had to run away. So I didn't want to stay with my parents. Mum and Dad were extremely good and understanding. That wouldn't do. Even my neighbours, who knew all about my deep desires to be a nun, couldn't believe I had left the convent. I had to get away. I chose to go to one of my brothers' places, in Makutano, about 50 km east of Mavoko. Andryn, the brother just younger to me, had a large farm there that gave me space to wander around in the plantations, lost in my thoughts. It was a good cooling off period. It gave me time to reflect. I was also able to reconnect with my great friend, Father Lucien.

He arranged for me to get to one of the institutions of the POS close to Mavoko. I re-trained and updated my computer skills even though I had to travel nearly two hours each way to the institution. Sometimes I walked back one way either going or coming back from classes. It gave me time to release all the pain within me. I was alright health-wise but by doing the computer packages I was not only re-qualifying myself, I was also gradually getting out of the depression that was slowly creeping in. I had almost blanked out of real living at one point but then slowly regained my questioning skills. I re-started my quarrels with the Lord.

'I can't believe the mess I'm in. Looks like You allowed it all to happen. Well, now that I'm there, get me out of it. You can see how hard I'm working.'

Six months down the line with some skills in the bag once again I got the help of another priest, Father Rowen, a friend of Father Lucien, who introduced me to an employer in need of a receptionist. Soon the company gave me some Accounts work as well. I suddenly found that my confidence was returning. So I continued getting into the workers' world and was there in employment for 8 years. That was truly the first blessing (in tangible human terms) that I hung on to after the Novitiate sending-away. My health too began to pick up and my financial situation improved slightly. I then decided I would attend college while working here, studying Accounts. In time I did a degree in Accounts. I moved on and did two more jobs, generally connected with Accounts and Secretarial work.

Quite suddenly all that ended in early 2012. Once more my faith was tested. I was diagnosed with cervical cancer and my bosses were a bit loath to take on my insurance claims. I had no choice. I had to leave before they could sack me, and then tried to find other ways to survive. The situation was a lot more complicated now. I now had my child, Faith, to care for as well. I resorted to my usual quarrels with the Lord.

'Now, why have You done this to me? I thought I was just about coping and this thing comes along and sort of upturns the apple cart. You never seem to amaze me with the games You play with me. I don't feel I'm prepared to face more disappointments. I'm not sure I can take it any longer.'

Yet there was no answer coming up. Somehow at the back of my head I knew that something would work out for me. In the hospital scans in late 2012 they found that the cancer was in remission. The doctors couldn't explain how I'd got the all-clear, but I knew that the herbal remedies I had placed my faith in had worked. (Or perhaps, it was the Lord getting back into my life.) So I couldn't but believe in them and I religiously stuck to this therapy. That strengthened my faith in them and gave me hope and confidence. So contrary to all medical opinions I could do without chemotherapy. I just had to go back for more negotiations in my quarrels.

'You've certainly got a hand in this. I'm beginning to see that, but You have to keep me alive for at least a decade. I want to see Faith through. I want to see her established. She has no one to care for her. I know You will understand. I have no one else to turn to. I know I can leave all my life's plans in your hands.'

I actually now live in this hope that I will be able to see my Faith through her studies. I will have completed the life cycle that every Akamba believes is the fulfilment of our life on earth: crossing all the thresholds to be where all the Akamba are gathered, a section of Heaven perhaps where we will all meet.

Quite strangely I have now had time to review my convent experiences. I find these have helped me mature a lot. I see them in a more positive light now. The joys and trials I went through have all prepared me for my life today. I might have cried a lot in my earlier years. I do not cry now. I am slowly beginning to realize that the Lord never abandoned me: He just knew what He was doing. Even the trials I had with Sister Joanna were possibly just some of His clever ways to bring me to where I am today. I think I now pray with greater belief and trust. Indeed I now believe I am beginning to live the holier life that Mum always wanted me to live. I am so glad that she is still alive to see me becoming a better Christian and to see Faith grow up. My Mum and Dad were such a large part of my life. I will never be able to thank them enough.

I seem to know how to cope and am trying to get my beloved Faith to try and understand the inscrutable ways of the Lord. I seem to have grown closer to the Lord. My quarrels with Him have in a strange kind of way brought me closer to Him. I'm now convinced, if I had any doubts earlier, that He'll stay the course with me. Those cancer drugs choked me. Now I'm not on these drugs and I feel better. In fact in one of my recent dreams I found myself at heaven's entrance with one of the saints, or is it angels, sort of telling me, 'There's time yet. You don't have to get in just now. We'll give you a 'Late Entry' ticket. Get back and do what you have to do. You have Faith now: just bring her up to speed.'

Chapter 12: A time to love...and for peace : Epilogue

Time has now rolled on. It is the year 2025 and I am now a little more mature than I was when I left the convent. I am still without a steady job but yet with some income from projects I had worked on earlier. My child, Faith, is now about to complete her University degree. She has matched up to her seniors, my brothers and sisters, in the academic world, and is a self-assured, reasonably mature Graduate-to-be in Psychology from the University of Nairobi. She is dating an Mzungu [white man] from South Africa, Jason. He's a project manager, working with UNESCO, who regularly visits Kenya for short stays, to oversee the progress and development of his plans. By a strange coincidence he had come to do a short one-year project at Nairobi University where he was charmed by none else than my beautiful daughter, Faith. Even though he is Methodist they plan on having a Catholic wedding, and that of course for someone like me, a stickler for traditional values, is immense relief.

Jason, who drives a Toyota, took us, Faith and myself, to the top floor of the Intercontinental hotel in what Americans would call 'downtown' Nairobi. It was Faith's 18th birthday, and she was on the threshold of her Graduation. She was in a chatty mood, and I was quite relaxed. So she thought she'd use the opportunity to get some answers to a few questions she'd be dying to ask me.

'Mum, you know what? I want to ask you some questions.'

'Questions? What sort of questions?' I was curious to know. I had noticed that of late she was keen on finding out details of the time she was still a child. I tried never to hide the truth from her.

'Well, some stuff of my childhood days. You think you can answer them?'

'I'll try,' I said, which was always my answer, because young as she was she had the style of an investigative journalist, and I was not really comfortable in being cross-questioned, not certainly by my own daughter. I guess I was cornered, and I had to put on a brave face.

'Going back to the time when you were pregnant with me: were you pleased, sorry or angry?'

'That's a difficult one. I don't think I was any of those. Really I was just plain worried. It was my first pregnancy and in the great Akamba tradition I almost felt privileged to be pregnant. But I also knew there were hazards. I was proved right later because you were born prematurely, and that of course caused a lot of anxiety.'

'Pretty good answer,' said Jason.

'OK. How about my father? Why hasn't he shown up all these years? Have you kept in touch? Is he aware that he caused you quite a few problems?' she queried.

'This is a more difficult one. I can't answer for him, as to why he hasn't shown up. But I did try to keep in touch. I did my best, because I wanted you to come to know your father...Yes a lot of problems came up but I think I've been able to cope with them.'

'So, you actually tried to contact him?'

'Yes, I did.'

'Any idea of where he is now or what has happened to him? Or why he has not kept in touch? Is he not interested in his own daughter?'

'I don't really know. I wish I had a better answer for you, my dearest.... Folks in our village say he's somewhere in Zimbabwe.'

'Fair enough. Perhaps it's best we leave him there. But I'm interested in some other news about the family.'

'And what is that?'

'I know you don't want to talk of Antyn, my uncle, who shattered us all when he left us. All I want to know is if you have come to terms with it. As for me I wasn't born then, and only picked up bits and pieces of what might have been the circumstances. Maybe, on another occasion you can talk to me about him, because he was so dear to you. I feel it is best we leave that for today.'

'Sounds good to me. Yes, perhaps another day would be good to talk about Antyn.'

'Yes, I too would like to know more about it,' said Jason.

'I'm actually more eager to know about those nuns in your life. I know you spoke so lovingly of Sabine to me one day. But you never seem to talk about Sister Joanna. She really did you a lot of harm, and yet you never speak against her. She really ruined your life. You might have been a good nun in a convent (and I might never have been born of course). She shattered all that. How have you taken that?'

'Somehow we Akamba do not take revenge or harbour hard feelings. Also my mum taught me to respect nuns and priests. I think I was shattered but I took it in my stride. It was painful. It was hard. It was in many ways disastrous. But my family, especially my

Mum and Dad supported me. My brothers and sisters were superb. I can never thank my family enough for all their love and care. All that helped me to forget all the pain Sister Joanna caused me.'

'Did you wish evil to come to her?'

'Nothing of the sort. I feel that if she has done wrong, she would have to answer to God at some point.'

'Do you know where she is now? Or, what has become of her?'

'Funny enough, without my trying to find out anything I was told by one of my Novitiate mates that the year after she sent me packing the nuns sent her back to Italy as she had gone in for a nervous breakdown. Actually it was something more serious as well: Alzheimer's it seems.'

'So, do you feel justified now? Do you think that was her punishment?'

'No, dear one, only God can mete out punishment or reward us. I do not wish her evil. On the contrary I wish she could recover and continue to do some good work. Maybe she had a lot of problems and I became the catalyst, and in some ways the victim of a poor decision.'

'You've not changed, Mum: always so kind and forgiving. I think she deserved what she got,' said Faith with a slight tinge of vindictiveness.

'I may not agree with you here,' I said. 'But I do know from messages I got recently that her last year in the novitiate was horrendous. The novices nearly went into revolt as she kept making ridiculous decisions and also acting in weird ways. She bungled a whole lot of managerial procedures, and the bosses had to transfer her in the middle of the novitiate year to another convent for rest and recovery. She had become a nervous wreck. Soon after that she developed medical complications, including a tumour in her brain, I think.'

'Don't you think the nuns owe you some sort of compensation?' Jason asked.

'That's not for me to ask or think of. But I do think they need to improve their procedures, and to have more than one person involved in decision making,' I said. 'Also, maybe people who have to handle lives like the Novices need more patience, and a lot of special training and updating.'

'Fair enough, from what you say,' said Jason once more. 'But in today's professional world your Sister would have come under fire, and maybe more.'

'Oh, let's leave the nuns alone,' Faith interrupted. 'Now, how about that guy we met last week?'

'Whom are you talking about?'

'Now, don't pretend Mum. I know you like him. It's Reuben, the head chef at Marriott's.'

'Oh, him? Well, we're good friends. It's nothing serious.'

'How can you say that? I've seen you texting him every day,' she continued.

'Now, now, you're intruding into my privacy, you naughty little devil,' I said somewhat annoyed.

'Well not really, but I happened to pick up a call from him on your phone when you were in the bath last evening....He clearly said *Ask Anna to call me back, please.* I gave you that message, and you did look a bit embarrassed when I did. Now, don't you like him?'

'Now, can we talk about something else?'

'But if you like him, just get on with it, Mum. We'll be so pleased for you.'

'Thanks for the thought anyway, sweetie. I'll keep you informed, if that's what you want.'

'Not just informed. Get going. Move on. We live life just once. You deserve all that's best.'

'Perhaps, if all goes well,' Jason chipped in, 'we might celebrate two weddings together.'

'Great idea,' Faith chimed in.

'Well, that might be good, if it happens,' I sort of chuckled, and felt a bit emboldened to add, 'I might then invite all my novice-mates to the wedding and perhaps some of the SOS nuns too, especially the ones I knew (if they're still around).'

'Sounds great, Mum,' said Faith apparently pleased with my answer.

We soon found it was near midnight and we were the last ones in the restaurant. 'Waiter,' I called out. 'Get us the bill.'

'I'm paying,' said Jason.

'Maybe we can go Dutch,' said Mum.

'No, this is my treat for Faith and for you Ana. You're both so wonderful. You especially have come such a long way, through such an incredible journey in life. You've more than survived: you've achieved. You've done a wonderful job in seeing Faith come so far. I feel privileged to have Faith in my life. And I feel lucky to be your son-in-law. It's my privilege to clear the bill.'

'Yes, Mum,' said Faith, 'just let him get on with it. He had better get used to bills and check-outs....It will remind him that he's also got to get me a dress for the Convocation!'

The End

114

GLOSSARY

***Active Orders**: These are different from Contemplative Orders because they do works of charity in schools, hospitals and elsewhere. They are also known as 'mendicant' Orders and their followers are also known as 'monks' as opposed to 'friars' for the Contemplative Orders.

***Agnes**: A Roman Saint who suffered martyrdom for her faith/religion at the age of only 13.

***Akamba**: The name of the tribe/clan that Anastasia belongs to. *Kikamba* is the Akamba language.

***Anastasia**: Saint: born of a Roman [pagan] father and a Christian mother. She was a friend of Saint Chrysogonus.

***Anglicans**: A Christian group that is Protestant.

***Apostles**: The 12 men chosen by Christ to be His closest followers like his inner Cabinet. Judas was one of them. He betrayed Christ to the Jewish religious leaders who had Him crucified later.

***Bantu**: It means 'people' and refers to the many tribes in West Africa, mainly in Nigeria, who moved east or south with their cattle and possessions, in migratory groups, either fleeing from the frequent droughts (in this South Saharan region) or from constant tribal squabbles. They traded as they moved along, generally eastwards. The language they used for communication came to be known as 'Bantu'. Many African languages have Bantu roots, including Kiswahili and Kikamba.

*Baptised Christian: Person who has had Baptism.

*Baptism: The Catholic initiation rite that makes a person a Catholic. It is a religious ceremony in which a person is sprinkled with water or immersed in water to symbolize purification. In some Christian Baptisms the person is named as well.

*Bernadette: Bernadette Soubirous: At the age of 18 this Saint had visions of Mary, Mother of Christ, at Lourdes, in France, which has now become a place of international pilgrimage.

*Bishop: A person in charge of a Diocese (or administrative district) for Christians/Catholics.

*Black Magic: Magic attempted for evil purposes, calling upon evil spirits or the devil.

*Brother (or Religious Brother): A man who commits himself to live in Community, and takes 3 vows: to live poor, to obey the religious laws of the Order and to agree to stay celibate, i.e. not to marry. This person does not become a Priest. Inversely, a Priest can be a 'Religious' as well, e.g. the priests in the White Fathers, the Comboni , the Consolata or the POS.

*Cardinal: A person, usually an Archbishop, who is one of the close advisers of the Pope, and is a member of the Conclave that elects a new Pope.

*__Canon__: most sacred and important part of the Catholic Mass.

*__Catholic__: One of the largest of the Christian denominations, with over a billion followers worldwide, with the Pope in Rome [in Vatican City] as the worldwide Head/Leader. Catholicism was the first group of Christian Churches (believers), and was founded by Christ himself. Catholic also means 'universal'.

*__Catholic Liturgy__: The rites used by Catholics for worship and prayer, especially in community.

*__Charismatic__: A Christian group characterized by a quest for inspired and ecstatic experiences such as healing, prophecy and speaking in tongues.

*__Christ__: Jesus Christ, born of Mary, who Christians believe is God, who came to redeem Mankind.

*__Christian__: Follower of Christ as a Catholic or as a Protestant.

*__Christening__: Another term for Baptism, which makes a person a 'Christian' or a follower of Christ.

*__Chrysogonus__: A Saint who was martyred by Emperor Diocletian. He was a priest-friend and adviser to Saint Anastasia, and a friend of Anastasia's mother, Saint Fausta.

*__Cinderella__: A children's folktale heroine who experiences a magical change of lifestyle, after a time of deprivation and servitude. She gets to dance with a Prince and to enjoy happiness and privilege.

*Circumcision: A controversial issue, especially between 1929 and 1932, when British Protestant groups tried to eradicate the practice from Kenya. This rite of passage for girls (FGM- female genital mutilation) lingered on till the 1960s, and is still there in some pockets of Kenyan/African society.

*Comboni : A religious Order that does charitable work, through parishes and community projects. They have male and female sections to their organization.

*Conclave: The sacred gathering of Cardinals empowered to elect a Pope, the head of the Catholics.

*Confession: The practice where a Catholic person goes to a priest to 'confess' his/her sins and then gets pardon or absolution.

*Consolata: A religious Order very much like the Comboni, the White Fathers, or the POS.

*Contemplative Orders: (see Active Orders): Also known as 'cloistered' Orders, where men or women stay permanently behind 'closed' doors: to be able to pray and meditate without any distraction. Many Orders also have strict rules and do not allow communication in conversation.

*Convent: A community of women living a life devoted to prayer and religious worship. Also, a building or premises occupied by a community of religious women.

*Danny Boyle: See Slumdog Millionaire.

*Daughters of Mary: (DOM): An Order of Nuns. (This is the Author's choice of an alternative name for an existing Order)

*Diocese: An administrative district formed by a few Parishes, with a Bishop in charge.

*Diocletian: Roman Emperor who systematically persecuted Christians for nearly 8 years. It is ironical that Christianity became Rome's official religion just after his death in 324 AD.

*Embu: A town north east of Nairobi, sort of half-way between Nairobi and Meru. (See Map)

*Evangelicals: See Pentacostalism.

*Evil Eye: It is a piercing look that conveys strong feelings of hatred, disapproval, jealousy or malice or that supposedly can cause harm. It also refers to a supernatural or magical power that some people in many cultures believe can bring harm or cause bad luck. The evil eye is usually given to others who remain unaware. Children are often made to wear amulets to ward off the evil eye.

*Friar: a man belonging to a Catholic religious Order. (See also: Monk & Active Orders).Some of the main

Orders who are Friars are: Augustinians, Carmelites, Dominicans and Franciscans.

*Gospels: The 4 books of the New Testament [about Christ & Christianity], that are part of the Bible. The word 'Gospel' means 'Good News'.

*Habit: Long loose gown, usually black, brown, grey or white, worn by nuns, friars and monks.

*Herodias: She was married a second time to Herod Antipas [4 BC- 39AD], ruler of Galilee in the time of Christ. John the Baptist, Christ's contemporary, openly criticized her incestuous marriage, and she had her revenge by getting him beheaded. The incidents are mentioned in the Gospels [Bible].

*Holy Family: The family of Jesus (Christ), Mary (mother of Jesus) and (Saint) Joseph.

*Holy Orders: Taking Holy Orders, i.e. being 'ordained'/made a Priest, in the Catholic Church.

*Idi Amin: Idi Amin Dada: dictator of Uganda. He forcefully took over the country from President Obote in 1971. His 6-year reign brought in economic decline, social disintegration and massive human rights violations. More than 300,000 were murdered during his reign of terror.

*Joan of Arc: Known as the Maid of Orleans: at 19 she led France to victory in the 100 years war, for Charles VII, but was later burnt at the stake as a witch, under English Bishops. She is a Saint featuring in books, plays and songs across the world. She is one of the Patrons of France.

*John Mbiti: John Samuel Mbiti is a Kenyan-born Christian religious philosopher and writer. He is an ordained Anglican priest, and since 2005 a Canon. He studied in Uganda, the USA and the UK. He taught religion and theology in Uganda and was director of the World Council of Churches in Switzerland. Mbiti's seminal book, *African Religions and Philosophy* (1969), was the first work to significantly challenge Christian assumptions that traditional African religious ideas were 'demonic and anti-Christian'. His interpretation of these religions is from a firmly Christian perspective.

*John the Baptist: Contemporary of Christ, who preached repentance to prepare people for the coming of Christ, the Saviour, as believed by Christians.

*Joseph in the Bible: Joseph, the 11th of 12 sons of Jacob (Book of Genesis in the Bible), sold by his brothers, because of jealousy, later found favour with Pharaoh, to become his Governor of Egypt.

*Judas: One of the 12 Apostles. He betrayed Christ. (See Apostles)

*Kikamba: the language of the Akamba people.

*Kikuyu: the largest, and possibly the most powerful, tribe in Kenya, who played a dominant role in Kenya's freedom movement. It is also the name of the Language of the tribe.

121

***Kiswahili**: the language of the Swahili people. It has Bantu and Arabic influences in it.

***Last Supper**: The picture/painting where Christ is at the last meal with his 12 Apostles. There are notable versions of it by Leonardo da Vinci and other artists.

***Lead Kindly Light**: A hymn by John Henry Newman, 1833. The first verse reads:

Lead, Kindly Light, amidst the encircling gloom, Lead Thou me on!
    The night is dark, and I am far from home, Lead thou me on!
    Keep Thou me feet; I do not ask to see- The distant scene; one step enough for me.

***LaVey**: LaVeyan Satanism is a philosophy (not considered a religion by many of its followers) was founded in 1966 by Anton Szandor LaVey. Its teachings are based on individualism, self-indulgence and 'eye for an eye' morality. Unlike Theistic Satanists, LaVeyan Satanists are atheists who regard Satan as a symbol of man's inherent nature. LaVeyan Satanism is believed to be a small group that is unrelated to any other faith, and its members feel free to satisfy their urges responsibly, exhibit kindness to their friends, and attack their enemies. LaVeyanism has influenced thinkers worldwide.

***Life of the Beloved**: by Henry Nouwen: It was initially written by the author for a Jewish friend, which soon became a best-seller. It was the author's legacy to Christians around the world.

*Liturgy: A form and arrangement of public worship prescribed by a Church or religion.

*Lourdes: Our Lady of Lourdes. Mary appeared to Bernadette Soubirous, a peasant girl, in this town in France in 1858. She was made a Saint later. It is one of the larger sites of pilgrimage for Catholics. Many miracles and cures are believed to take place here.

*Lucy: A Roman Saint martyred during Emperor Diocletian's reign as she refused to marry the pagan governor of Syracuse (Sicily). Probably because her eyes were gouged out she is venerated as patroness of the blind.

*Machakos: a large town in Kenya, heartland of the Akamba, south of Nairobi, the capital. (See map)

*Maria Goretti: An Italian virgin-martyr of the Roman Catholic Church. She is one of its youngest canonized saints, at 12. She died from multiple stab wounds inflicted by her attempted rapist after she refused to submit to him.

*Mass: The most sacred function in the Liturgy of Catholics: where bread and wine are transformed symbolically (and realistically in Catholic belief) into Christ's body and blood. Important parts of the Mass include the Bible Readings, the Offertory procession, the Canon and the Eucharistic Prayer. Catholics are expected to attend Mass at least once a week, possibly on Sundays.

***Mavoko**: A town in Kenya, south of Nairobi, the capital. (See map of Kenya).

***Meru**: A town in Kenya, far north east of Nairobi. (See map of Kenya)

***Methodists**: One of the Christian groups. (See also Protestant.)

***Monk**: A holy person, man or woman; generally a priest. (See also: Friar & Active Orders)

***Mother Teresa**: Of Albanian origin, originally belonging to the Loreto Order of Nuns. She founded the Missionaries of Charity, in Kolkata, India, to work for poor and abandoned people. The Order now has hospices and centres across the world, and over 2500 followers, women and men.

***Mount Kenya**: One of Kenya's highest mountains: at 5199 metres, at the Equator, 37E.

***New Testament**: See Gospels.

***Novice**: A prospective candidate who wants to enter religious life as a man or a woman.

***Novitiate**: It is the period of training (1 or 2 years) that a novice of a religious institute undergoes prior to taking Vows in order to discern whether s/he is called to Religious Life. (See Vows)

*Offertory: (procession): An important part of the Mass in the Catholic Liturgy.

*Order: A Catholic religious group or organization that does voluntary, charitable work through institutions like schools, parishes, youth centres, hospitals and community projects.

*Ordination: The function where a Bishop anoints a lay person to become a Catholic Priest.

*Our Lady....: A title given to Mary, the mother of Christ, e.g. Our Lady of Lourdes.

*Pagan: A religious adherent who does not follow one of the world's main religions, or a follower of an ancient polytheistic or pantheistic religion, or one who has no religion at all.

*Parish: An area or small administrative district with people who are Catholic or Christian, and who are ministered to by their Pastor, or Parish Priest. A group of Parishes form a Diocese.

*Parish Council: The leading people elected in a Catholic Parish who assist the Parish Priest to make decisions for the Parish.

*Parish Priest: A Catholic Priest responsible for a Catholic Parish.

*Pentecost: A Christian festival that commemorates the coming of the Holy Spirit upon the Apostles, or the day on which it is celebrated, i.e. 50 days (Pente- in Greek) after Easter.

*Pentecostalism: One of the Protestant Churches, which believes in the unerring power of the Bible and of the Gospels. The followers are often known as Evangelicals (Greek word for Gospel follower). The movement took roots in western USA in the 1900s. Believers are often asked to be 'born again' (or get a Baptism again) to be truly inserted into the Church.

*Pilate: Pontius Pilate: Governor of Judea in Israel, during the time of Christ. He symbolically washed his hands to signify that he wouldn't have anything to do with the death of Christ. [AD 26-36]

*Pope: The head of the Roman Catholic Church based in the Vatican, in Rome, Italy.

*Postulant: Somebody who applies to join a religious Order; one in the early stages of training.

*Presbyterianism: It is one of the Protestant Churches, based on Calvinism, founded in Scotland. It believes in a 'conciliar' approach to decision making, and theoretically there are no Bishops. Most decisions are taken by elected representatives of the people and of the clergy.

*Priest: One who owes allegiance to and works under a Bishop, among Catholics, and agrees to live celibate, i.e. does not marry.

*Priests of the Slums (POS): An Order that works for the education of underprivileged young people in many parts of Africa. (POS is the Author's choice of an alternative name for an existing Order).

*Protestant: A member or adherent of any denomination of the Christian Church that rejects the authority of the Pope and some fundamental Catholic doctrines, and believes in justification by faith. The formulation of Protestants' beliefs began with the Reformation in the 16th Century. A Protestant could be Anglican, Methodist, Presbyterian, Lutheran, Mormon, Pentecostal, or a member of any one of the over 30,000 Church groups in the world today.

*Retreat: A period away from normal activities, devoted to prayer and meditation, often spent in a religious community.

*Rite of Passage: Individuals, men and women, have to go through these traditional practices in Kenyan (& generally African) society, when they are young, to become accepted members of adult society. (See also Circumcision)

*Saint: A holy person whose life has been outstanding and who after death is proclaimed as such by the Pope, in the Catholic Church.

*Saint Anthony: Anthony of Padua, also known as Anthony of Lisbon, was a Portuguese Catholic priest and friar of the Franciscan Order. Though he died in Padua, in Italy, he was born and raised in a wealthy family in Lisbon. He is venerated around the Catholic world as a patron of lost things and generally a great friend of the poor and the needy. His legendary status as a great miracle worker has in a way obscured his real personality as a truly learned man and teacher.

*Sermon: A talk at a religious function, or on a religious topic, at a Catholic Liturgy.

*Servant of God: The first stage in the process towards making a Catholic holy person a Saint in the Catholic Church. The next stages are: Beatification (Blessed) and Canonization (Saint).

*Sister: a name for a female person who dedicates her life to the service of others, and who has to take 3 Vows: to live poor, to obey the Order's laws and not to marry; and lives in a community.

*Sister Act: A film: When a worldly singer witnesses a mob crime, the police hide her as a nun in a traditional convent where she has trouble fitting in. Whoopi Goldberg stars.

*Sisters of Christ (SOC): An Order that works mainly in Parishes and Centres to spread the Gospel message through preaching and distributing the printed word in many countries of Africa. (SOC is the Author's choice of an alternative name for an existing Order).

*Slumdog Millionaire: A film by UK director Danny Boyle, winner of Bafta and Academy awards, where a boy from the Mumbai slums wins the Indian version of 'Who wants to be a millionaire'.

Sound of Music: A film set in the 1930s, where Maria, a postulant, is given a break from her convent chores to test her genuine intentions of being a nun. She works as a governess for a family and then actually falls in love with Baron Von Trapp, the head of the family. (Julie Andrews stars.)

Swahili: The ethnic group of people and culture found in East Africa of about 60 million people, who live on the east coast of Tanzania, Kenya, and Mozambique as well as on the islands in the area, from Zanzibar to Comoros, who speak Swahili (or Kiswahili). One-fourth of Africa speaks Swahili.

Synaxaria: Collections of short lives of Saints or Holy People, maintained in the Community.

Teresa of Avila: Spanish Catholic Saint. She is considered to be a leading Doctor of the Church.

Theology: The study of God and Religion: referred to here as the 4 years of study required by candidates who want to become Catholic Priests.

Therese of Lisieux: French nun who became a Saint at 24, who influenced a younger generation to holiness by the simplicity of her life, or as she called it, her 'little way' to sanctity.

Vows: These are solemn, public promises made by members of Catholic Religious Orders to become members of the Orders. These are mainly to live Poor, to remain Celibate and Obedient to the laws of the Order. They also promise to live in Community. These

Vows are first taken for 1 or for 3 years (Temporary), and then Permanently (Final). (See also 'Brother')

*White Fathers: A religious Order like the Comboni and the Consolata, who work all over Africa.

REVIEWERS' BACKGROUNDS

Beena Menon: Beena, is a Training Consultant for Teacher Education for the British Council in India. She has worked as Language Trainer for Chiang Mai Rajabhat University Thailand and as Head of Languages for KIIT University, Orissa, India. She also delivers lectures on ESOL Development and on Teaching to different organizations in India, and helps develop training programmes for students at college and university level.

Bia Menezes: Bia is a Certified School Library and Media Specialist and works in a NYC school. In addition to her B.A. and her B. Ed she holds an M.A. and an M.L.S (in Library Studies). She was formerly employed by the New York Public Library where she reviewed books for the Library Branch collection. She now continues with her work developing her school library collection.

Fred Gomes: Fred has been a successful teacher of English and Drama in Queensland, Australia, for over twenty years, after a successful career over a decade as a teacher in Senior School in Saint Joseph's and in La Martinere, Kolkata, and later in Jamshedpur, India, as a well-known lecturer for B Ed in Loyola, for Communications in XLRI, TATA Management Training Centre and for Linguistics in Cooperative College. He now teaches Ballroom Dancing and tours Australia and New Zealand as a Ballroom Dancing specialist, judging contests. He has worked in institutions run by three different religious Orders and is familiar with how they conduct their training. He keeps up with trends in writing, drama, music and dancing.

Joe Thomson: Joe has several years' experience of youth and project work in East Africa. He set up programmes for young people in vocational schools to develop their skills for employment. He also does counselling sessions for families and for adults. His uses his financial and administrative expertise in constantly improving training programmes that benefit young people. His reading helps him keep abreast of trends in youth training and education as well as in areas connected with counselling, administration and management.

Joseph P Lazar: Joseph has spent his career as Counsellor, Advisor to adults and young people both in career choices as well as in personal support. His specialist fields include developing programmes in religious instruction and personal development. Joseph trained in Europe and in India, and has played a significant role in the lives of many young people who have gone on to become leaders in religious organizations or as adult Christian leaders who now hold responsible positions in society. Joseph himself has spent many years in taking on managerial and pastoral roles in leading Christian institutions in East Africa.

Paul D'Souza: Paul spent over a decade teaching Senior Students in Saint Joseph's in Kolkata, India, before moving to Toronto's Education Board placements. He distinguished himself as a teacher both in his dedication to work and to supporting students in their examination schedules and in their career choices. In retirement he and his wife, Lena, are involved in socio-religious projects for adults and families where they act as counsellors and animators. Paul finds time to read widely and keeps abreast of developments in religious, educational and social areas. He and Lena also travel a lot in America, Asia and Europe because they love people and enjoy travelling.

Phil Matthews: Phil has directed programmes for families and groups in India over several years, involving Christian teaching and practical psychology in his sessions. He also has under his belt many years of experience as a teacher, manager and trainer. He has educational qualifications from Europe and from India and has specialized in programmes for young people going into employment and those preparing to enter or in training in religious Orders. He keeps in touch with the latest trends in youth training and employment as well as in education, management and counselling.

Sabita Nazareth: Sabita has had a flourishing teaching career in leading Christian schools in Mumbai, India, for nearly three decades, generally in 'convent' High Schools. Her desire to be able to serve others with the skills she had took her into drama, public speaking and choreography in Church groups and in the community. Besides her Masters in History and her PG Dip in Management of Education she was also given the prestigious Rotary Club award for her thesis on 'Teacher Absenteeism and Indiscipline in Schools'. She uses her fluency in several languages to give vocational guidance to students and counselling to adults and families. She keeps up with the latest trends in reading and also contributes occasionally to local journals.

Xavier Pinto: Xavier, who has a Commerce degree, has won awards in Hospitality and Tourism from Ryerson University, Toronto, Canada. He was selected as a top expert by Ontario Hostelry Institute for his work with student researchers. He featured in the Ted Rogers School of Hospitality as 'one of the faces of the future'. He also volunteers as a Medical Escort for disabled people and offers tennis coaching to over 200 enthusiasts of all ages. He reads widely and is interested in trends in published writing as well as in technological development today.

THE AUTHOR

Trophy D'Souza has published two books on dysfunctional situations: 1, on religious Managers who malfunction (*A Bumpy Ride*); 2, on a family that has problems settling into normal functioning (*The Singh Saga*). This book, 3, (*Anastasia Redeemed*) is again about religious Managers who need to appreciate that they need to bring empathy and the human touch to dealing with human problems, (e.g. understanding and support), and not high-handed stitch-ups, to suit targets of the Order or subjective interests of its Managers.

His books bring out his wealth of experience as a manager, teacher, youth-worker and education advisor in Asia, Europe and Africa. His work and interaction also with men and women of different religious Orders have helped him gain insights into their training and lifestyle, which have stood him in good stead in the writing of two of his books, 1 and 3. Now based in the UK he conducts English Language courses and projects and writes life stories. He occasionally contributes to sports, music, drama, literary and news blogs. The Quantified Assessments he designed, used by departments of two colleges in the UK and two in India, are typical of the objective approach he takes to people and situations.

Trophy brings to his writing his captivating style of language, packed with humour, wit and information, which also reflects his interests in drama, music, history, culture and literature (areas he has been involved in during his career), as well as his work and travel experiences in different countries.

REFERENCES

1. The Symbol '®' used after words or phrases in the text indicates that there is an explanation to them in the Glossary.

2. The Protagonist, Anastasia, is in many ways a real person. The Author gets her to tell her story in her own words.

3. Most references and background details are from Wikipedia Websites.

4. The Chapter headings are from the Bible, from the Book of Ecclesiastes, Ch 3: Vs 1 to 8:

Time for Everything

<u>1</u>There is a time for everything, and a season for every activity under heaven:

<u>2</u>a time to be born and a time to die, a time to plant and a time to uproot,

<u>3</u>a time to kill and a time to heal, a time to tear down and a time to build,

<u>4</u>a time to weep and a time to laugh, a time to mourn and a time to dance,

<u>5</u>a time to scatter stones and a time to gather them, a time to embrace and a time to refrain,

6a time to search and a time to give up, a time to keep and a time to throw away,

7a time to tear and a time to mend, a time to be silent and a time to speak,

8a time to love and a time to hate, a time for war and a time for peace.

MAP of KENYA

Map of Kenya: courtesy of Wikipedia

www.ingramcontent.com/pod-product-compliance
Lightning Source LLC
Chambersburg PA
CBHW030131260626
47156CB00008B/2899